TRIBUTES TO TORONTO

BIN SOBCHUK

TRIBUTES TO TORONTO

iUniverse books may be ordered through booksellers or by contacting:

iUniverse
1663 Liberty Drive
Bloomington, IN 47403
www.iuniverse.com
844-349-9409

Because of the dynamic nature of the Internet, any web addresses or links contained in this book may have changed since publication and may no longer be valid. The views expressed in this work are solely those of the author and do not necessarily reflect the views of the publisher, and the publisher hereby disclaims any responsibility for them.

Any people depicted in stock imagery provided by Getty Images are models, and such images are being used for illustrative purposes only.
Certain stock imagery © Getty Images.

ISBN: 978-1-6632-6452-7 (sc)
ISBN: 978-1-6632-6453-4 (e)

Library of Congress Control Number: 2024913695

Print information available on the last page.

iUniverse rev. date: 07/17/2024

Contents

1   I Love the Toronto Police Force...1

2   Queen Elizabeth II Tributes 5

3   Halloween Cats..9

4   Special Boyfriend 11

5   Diva...13

6   Milo...15

7   Dear Sir Mayor John II 19

8   Doctor Wood..21

9   The Girl I Met..23

10   My New Boyfriend..25

11   The Toronto Transit Commission....................................27

12   Daddy's Belt..29

13   Dates...31

14   Crisis...33

15   Father Ted...35

16   Bo Comes Back..39

17   Beresford Avenue Yard Sale 41

18   Campaign US President Joe Biden 43

19   King's Noodle Restaurant 45

20   Fingerprint...47

21   My Beloved Husband..49

22   Nina and Q...51

23 One Night's True Adventure 55

24 51 Division M Hayford 57

25 Banknote 2 59

26 My Home 61

27 Anthony Fahy 65

28 It's the Simple Things 69

29 The Next Generation 71

30 The Good TTC Driver 73

31 Mervyn Johnston and I 75

32 Housing and Construction 79

33 The Black Girl 81

34 Broadview Hotel 83

35 Doctor Devanshu Desai 87

36 I am Daddy's Little Doggy 89

37 Mervyn Johnston 91

38 Hot Apollo 95

39 Buddy's Birthday 97

40 Dr. Wood's Retirement 99

41 China Chin Hot Pot and BBQ Toronto 101

42 Halloween Cats II 103

43 Pable Picasso 111

44 Stephen Goodwin's Biography 113

45 The TTC Night Bus 115

46 Police 12 Division Community Activity 117

47 Wok & Roast Chinese BBQ Restaurant 121

48 My English Teacher Michael 123

49 My Beloved Husband 127

50 The Underworld Fight with the Police 129

I Love the Toronto Police Force

As a long-time immigrant in this city of immigrants, I can honestly say—without wanting to sound boastful—that I have experienced a lot. One earlier experience during my time in the big city will serve to illustrate not only the diversity of what I have been through, but also show my readers, perhaps, that even when we may feel as if we're behind the eight ball, that proverbial black ball need not run over us. Case in point: The Toronto Police. They may have made me angry before, but I love them now.

In the early stages of my marriage, my ex-husband–like virtually every couple, I realize–had our ups and downs. But in our case, this is putting it mildly. There was great passion in our relationship which made the highs ecstatically wonderful, but this passion was equally intense in times of dispute. But on one late-summer evening in the sixth year of our marriage, I feared the anger between us had boiled over to the point where the risk of serious physical harm to one of us was actually a real possibility. On this particular occasion I wasn't taking any chances. I dialed 911 and the panic in my voice must have made the necessary impression on the operator, because in short order the police had arrived at our home.

After entering the living room and assessing the situation (at least one eyebrow was raised, I perceived, at the torn-up pillows on the sofa and the turned over lazyboy), to my surprise, they ended up arresting me. The police said that neighbours had alleged that I had been the instigator of physical violence toward my better half. I protested. *Did they not know what energetic cats can do to furniture?!* Okay, to be fair, my husband was not exactly a big guy, and I am a rather robust youngish woman, but my feelings were that, in spite of the heated rhetoric and even shoving between the two of us, it had been at least an equal exchange of vehemence, and that I had not been the more aggressive. However, at the time I couldn't help but feel the police were discriminating against me based on my Chinese ethnicity (my husband was white) and I was a Chinese Canadian. I ended up going to jail for over one month. In jail, I have to admit, I wasn't entirely unhappy. They provided rather tasty–if not rather calorie-laden–food, so good that, at times, I found it hard to believe that I was behind bars *(Is our cook moonlighting at Earls or something?).* What's more, I had a room all to myself and, at times, I slept like a log. Maybe it was the missing tension. Anyway, all in all, I was satisfied with this arrangement. And this experience set a chain of events in motion that ended with me, eventually, divorcing my husband. Probably better for both of us, when considered from a pragmatic perspective.

After that, I moved in with a Cantonese family, but I didn't find them to be the kindest of landlords. They often quarrelled with me and sometimes fought with me–once again, in fact, the police found their way into my home. The family were a tight unit of four and, being by myself once again, this only intensified my feeling of loneliness. It was as if I couldn't catch a break, trouble following me like a rollercoaster without brakes. I ended up being up in jail several times within those two years. After one arrest, in particular, I felt that I was actually in danger. On a windy early-spring morning, I found myself in the back of a squad car heading to the hospital. Perhaps it was the accumulating incidents resulting in a panic attack, maybe it was the wacky March weather, but, quite inexplicably, I had a premonition that I would die. And nobody would witness it. I imagined my body rotting in the earth outside the hospital with nary a soul remembering my existence. So I said to the doctor: "If you feel that my body and organs could be useful, I would like to be a donor." Before long, I was surrounded by police officers–not in a confrontational way, rather they approached with the appearance of genuine concern. They spoke with the doctor who ultimately, in a sombre tone, asked them to take me to the psychiatric ward.

Another time, I was quite ill; my first thoughts were to visit the nearest police precinct to my home, the Toronto Police 14 Division, where I found the strangest words coming out of my mouth, "Kill Obama." No one laughed at me. Immediately, but instead just listened to me, eventually driving me back home in their police car. The police, as I look back on it now, were being reliable, just, and even compassionate. My first thought is always to trust them before (only) later having doubts. I love the police, although sometimes I think they could be nicer.

Yesterday, I called the police because my tenant swore at me and threatened me. One middle-aged, brown-haired police officer–one with a spare tire around his mid-section that I find strangely endearing–has helped me many times. I admit, I now care for him just as I would an older brother. In this case, he comforted me and talked to my tenant, who later apologized to me. I was not sure exactly how to show my thanks to him, so I gave him a silver coin. He said that he shouldn't take it, so I went back in the house. The next day, I opened my door and found that the coin was on my porch chair. I knew that he had returned it. Nevertheless, thanks to his simple acts of kindness, not to mention his seemingly limitless patience with me, my feeling at the time was that he was one of the best Toronto police officers I had ever met. Thank you to my police officer! I love you.

Toronto Chief of Police Myron Demkiw is a Canadian of Ukrainian descent. I am very proud of him. However, when he first became Toronto's Chief of Police, I disliked him. I felt the former chief James Ramer had been exceptionally kind, unassuming, and approachable. I had liked him very much and had hoped that he could have served another four years. The new chief, to my mind, appears to be overworked and overwhelmed. He seldom smiles. But when I found out about his achievements and his Ukrainian background, I began to really like him as well. He graduated from the University of Toronto with a master's degree and two bachelor's degrees and is intelligent and strong. As my former husband was also of Ukrainian ancestry, I admire Chief Demkiw even more.

Not to be outdone, the police superintendent, Tyrone Hilton, has won five medals. He is a highly ambitious and capable professional. I hope that he will be a Toronto deputy police chief and Toronto deputy mayor someday. Absolutely, he is a hero in my mind.

I love the Toronto Police Force—they are our heroes and heroines. We need them, not only to help us in our daily lives, but to make us want to become better as a city.

Queen Elizabeth II Tributes

Queen, in the linguistic sense, equates with *lioness.* I admired the late Queen Elizabeth II so much that I would have rubbed her feet.

I miss the Queen. I loved her Majesty and I *still* feel an allegiance to her, which may seem strange for someone born so far from any British Isle. But, as a naturalized Canadian citizen, I have, literally, sworn my loyalty to her, something that I had the opportunity to do at my citizenship ceremony. I suppose I took this moment to heart.

John, please turn on the light during the night, because the Queen misses us.

Queen, my lioness, your heritage speaks to the British Kingdom's dignity and power. You are my Queen. You are our Majesty and you will never die. You are our goddess forever. My Queen, my Worship, I wish I could be your servant—to serve you for good.

I am excited that our new king is the beloved first born son of this great lady. I hope he will reign over us with the same wisdom and generosity that his mother did.

I love tigers and I knew the Queen loved them too. The Toronto Zoo has many newborn tiger cubs; I wish the Queen could see them tonight. During her final hours, I thought, *Don't die. Please don't die. We all pray for you.* For me, she was the Queen of monarchs, with a history as bright as Venus. From her humble work as a vehicle mechanic during the War, to her willingness to visit people from all walks of life across the planet, in her life she did so much to set an example for, and inspire, the whole world. I loved her style.

Queen, for me, you are the greatest in the whole Royal Kingdom. We all salute you. Your way is as high as heaven, and your life is as long as a pharaoh's. Don't go; don't go. We need thee forever.

If you do not know much about Tibet, you may not know of King Gesar. You may not be familiar with the epic of King Gesar, the monarch who has the most tributes. I think that my Queen deserves these tributes as well, and I think of her as my mother forever. Really, in my view she has led us into a new era. As a show of reverence, I say, *her Majesty,* three times to show my respect and love for her.

Today, I've noticed there is not a full moon. As I look to the sky, I think that my dearest Queen will go to heaven to reign over her new kingdom. *Go successfully, my Queen. Queen, you are superior; you reached your goals and left us at a challenging time. We need you to show the Mufasa's, the king of lions, face to show your talents to all.*

For me, the British king is also the true symbol of our society. The Queen was our royal crown. She was the British Commonwealth's brightest star in Heaven, and, in a sense, her epic will live on. Many have depended on her for their well-being. We will love her forever. *Goodnight my Queen.*

Although she's gone, to me she is still my mother, a shining example of fairness and compassion, humility and service. She is my heroine and royal highness.

My Queen, the whole world remembers you, and because of you, I am aware that a woman also has the power to rule mankind. I love you and admire you for providing this inspiration.

Halloween Cats

Milo is my new kitty. He was born on August 20th, 2022. This is his first Halloween. This Halloween, there are three cats in my home, Prince, Bo and Milo. Bo will move out tomorrow, so this will be his last Halloween with us. I am not that busy, since outside it's raining—and COVID 19 is ravaging the planet. A lot of kids are at home from school, and the world, it feels, has taken an uneasy pause. I, however, feel so lucky, with my two black cats keeping me company and my troublemaker, Milo, running all over the house.

Tonight, I have bought a big box of chocolates and am waiting for the kids to come. One hour has passed and only a few children have shown up. Hence, I go back inside to please my cats. Prince always fights with Milo. Bo does not want me to cuddle him, and thus I am a little bit sad. I'm thinking that, perhaps, it's the last time I will play with him. *See you, Bo!* Prince is over ten years old, so now he is not as active as he was before. He lays on my carpet and purrs. Bo shakes his beautiful tail and *cat*walks across the living room. I call Bo, but he ignores me. Okay—let him be. Milo is a young scout, who loves running up and down the stairs and climbing everywhere. I feel dizzy just watching him. He is absolutely the naughtiest cat that I have ever met.

For Halloween, I had thought about buying them some costumes. Yet my budget is tight, so I did not buy them, which leaves me feeling sorry for them. I love black cats, whether it's Halloween or not. Even Milo has a black face, ears, paws, and tail. Love at first sight—you say that again for these three cats. To me, they are my babies and are gifts from God.

Besides Milo, the other two cats do not like to be held and kissed and Bo, having come back to me, is not that violent now. If he does not like what I do, he will sound out a "HA HA" to express his feelings. But I don't care; I know that this is my last chance to do so. Bo is not light anymore, being sixteen pounds and a heavy eater now. Prince gets his trick-or-treat cat snack. He warns the other cats not to come near him. Milo is very curious and always wants his full portion. *Sorry no more left, young fella.* Although Milo is eleven weeks old, very tidy, and just two pounds, he already can climb up and down the stairs.

I love my three cats and wish them a happy Halloween.

Special Boyfriend

I put an advertisement in the Toronto Star newspaper, to find a husband, five times. A lot of people replied to it. One man who is an electrical engineer called me and told me his personal information. He had experienced a miserable childhood; his parents and his grandma from his mother's side often beat him and his two sisters. He was whipped, caned, belted, and spanked etc. while nude. His siblings experienced the same abuse as well and were severely punished. He sometimes protected his older sister, who was punished more since she did not cry.

Now he has a stable income, and he owns a house and a car, is doing pretty well. He lives alone and has an interesting habit. When he comes home, he will take off all his clothes and is nude in the house. He enjoys this privacy. He invited me to his house and to do exactly the same thing that he does in the house. This caused me to hesitate. I had joined the Toronto Spanking Club for years, and like I English Discipline. I did have a long time without this experience, because my husband passed away. I was very excited about this new possibility, yet I was afraid of sexually transmitted diseases, which can be passed on by the tools that are used for punishment. I am a widow. If I got a sexual disease, people would immediately look down upon me. So in this case, I really did not know what I should do. He said that he had had three girlfriends who all accepted corporal punishment. I did not know if I should go through that or not.

This man is good at cooking. I cannot imagine that I would stand to eat or even sit down to eat after receiving his punishment.

Diva

Diva is an Italian lady whose birthday is in early January and is just a little bit older than my late husband. His birthday is on January 24th, 1949. They were classmates for thirteen years. They often joked with each other. Diva said that she wanted to marry my husband. Diva was married for over one year when her husband disappeared, and she never got him back or married any other person. She is very sad.

Diva is a barking dog—she is always against everybody. But also, she is kind, which is why I like her. Every time Diva, Mervyn and I go to restaurants to eat, Diva will fight with the restaurants' staff. We just tolerate her.

Diva is very lucky. Once she was hit by two cars; she was pushed up in the air and fell down flat onto the street. The drivers were scared and fled the scene. She was sent to the hospital, where everyone thought that she was going to die. They even put her on a stretcher on the floor. Finally, she woke up and stayed in the hospital for over two weeks, as she had broken four bones. We all visited her and helped her a lot. I also learned to cross the street at the pedestrian crosswalk.

Diva loves animals and birds and often feeds them. Her favorite animals are kittens, whether they are kitty cats or raccoons' babies. She hangs out with them all the time. Diva has a raccoon troops, and she can lead them to destroy a building. She feeds the birds with bread, sometimes finding leftovers in public garbage cans. Even I cannot do it. I will love her kindness forever. Diva loves my dog, whose name is Buddy. Perhaps this is why she invited her girlfriend, Barber, to teach me how to train and walk Buddy. Buddy is big, goofy, and stubborn, so he doesn't always follow orders. I feel pity for him.

Diva sometimes is very cheap, seldom treating me and Mervyn. She has a car, but she does not drive very often, preferring to walk to save money. Diva is beautiful and keeps herself well made up. I love her big and funny nose.

Diva worked for the TTC, Toronto Hydro, and for the Toronto Police Force for many years. She loved her jobs. Even today, she still calls her colleagues.

Diva has many good clothes, but she just wears them to her rich friends' parties. I never see them when Mervyn, she and I hang out together, making me think that she's a bit of a snob. Hence, sometimes I dislike her.

Milo

I adopted a kitty and named him Milo. My wish is that one day Buddy (my dog) will come back to me—I think they would be the best of friends. Milo is a handsome kitty with blue eyes and a black face, ears, paws and tail. I like him. Milo is a barking squirrel, with a funny face and always fighting to win. Milo can go into and onto many places, such as my bed, tables and sofa. He is the naughtiest kitty that I have met, despite being so tiny. He is just a little bit bigger than my hand. Light too. He is a very handsome Siamese cat. As his mom, I will love him forever. Milo is always hiding. Sometimes, I waste several hours trying to find him. In these instances, I'm exhausted and completely out of steam, but I do not blame him—I love him. Prince, my cat, is eager to watch Milo and walks around him. They do not fight often, which makes me feel very lucky. Milo got his Christmas gift – a fur mouse toy and treats. He fights with Prince to eat the treats.

One day, I put Milo on my bed and change the kitty litter box. It took less than five minutes to change it; when I turned around, he was gone. I tried my best to find him. I even lay on the floor looking under the bed. He was not there. I began to panic and called 911, to talk to Toronto fire for help, but they refused. I called the Toronto police but got no help. I was especially afraid of my one tenant, who loves the cats too, but sometimes abuses them. If Milo was in his hands, I feared I may never see him anymore. I pretended to be looking for his cat and ask him whether he saw Milo or not. I went to his door three times; all he said was no and, after a minute, closed the door. Sitting there by myself, I felt helpless and afraid. I had just had a big and pleasant surprise because of adopting Milo; now, sorrow was washing over me. Over three hours passed, and I begin to search under and around my bed again. I suddenly saw Milo hiding under the pillows. I smiled and held him while he went to sleep.

In the morning, I woke up and he was still sleeping beside me, confirming for me that I was a successful mom. Last night, my neighbour, who is a *Pet Value* owner, brought me a bag of kitten food for twenty dollars. Milo ate a chunk of barbequed pork as big as his head, as well as a piece of barbequed duck. He loved it. I also ordered a collar and name tag for him, which was worth almost thirty dollars. My endless love is for Milo.

Now Milo is part of my life and I think about him constantly. I booked a vet appointment for him on Saturday with my favourite veterinarian, Saini. Milo is bold and eager to discover everything. I know that Milo loves me; I know now that I loved him at first sight, my baby.

Prince, my other cat, is weird. He sometimes likes Milo and sometimes threatens Milo. Yet Milo does not care about this and does anything that he wants. I am his protector. Milo's scratches are very painful and can cause bleeding. He likes sleeping, often suddenly falling sleep for the whole day after a period of play. One time, Milo did not eat, pee, or poop for three days. I was very worried about him. Recently, I felt very upset. Milo always pees and poops on the mattress of my bed and on my quilts. There are some wet spots on them. Once, he even peed on my tenant's clothes. Sometimes he poops in the kitty litter boxes. He needs more training now.

Dear Sir Mayor John 11

In my mind, John is my big brother. I have admired him for a long time. He said that he likes me too. I think *sometimes I fear you because I love you; I fear to lose you because I need you; I fear your silence because I could lose my dearest; I fear long distance because I want you call me with local.* Love cannot be concealed; love is your gentle attentions; love is blind. Sometime for us, love is everything. For my brother John, my waiting time seems endless. My love is strong, and I need his feedback and love. I know that maybe I dream too much, but I just want gun to say, "I love you." to me.

John is a hard-working farmer. He wants to buy a hay harvest combine but does not have enough money even for a second hand one, which is worth 16,000 dollars. At the beginning, I tried to help him and sold some antiques in my house. Yet it was not enough. I wrote letters to Premier Doug Ford for help. He replied to me and suggested that I contact the Ontario Provincial Agricultural Administrator. She finally released the funds to him. He got over 60,000 dollars for a brand-new machine for which he was much appreciative.

We communicate about politics too. For Ukraine and Russian's war, we have an innovative solution. As the old saying goes, all roads lead to Rome. We decided that Italy's numerous and well-equipped ports could be used by Ukraine to ship their many agricultural products abroad. After all, if the EU countries are true allies they should be willing to help Ukraine in non-military areas as well as providing arms to defend themselves.

Once we talked about New Yorkers. I felt that they should not always think they are number one in the world. I am a Torontonian and am proud of it. John came into my home wearing NY pants, which irritated me at first. But I realized that this shouldn't bother me, and that there are good people everywhere. This experience taught me that we should not fight to win, and tolerance is very important. I cannot deny New Yorkers their glory.

Brother John adopted my dog, Buddy. Today I dreamed that Buddy had many puppies. Buddy was embarrassed. He and I held each other; he is just like a one-year-old boy doggie. I love all of them. *Buddy is your son now. I won't grab him from you, and I am just your dog's servant.* Now, I notice that John's clothes have dog smell. Every time he comes to my home, my cats immediately hide. Funny, right?

Brother John: I saw the photos of you and your father in your Facebook. I noticed your smiles, which makes you even more beautiful. Thank you!

Doctor Wood

Two years ago, I got moderate arthritis, which was very painful. My family doctor referred me to specialist, Doctor Michael Wood. He is very famous and professional. He always wears his operating uniform and running shoes and is of average height and build—but there's nothing average about his skill as a physician. He has a lot of patients. Additionally, he works in two hospitals and one private clinic. He likes drinking diet Coca-Cola, which I've noticed he drinks at work.

My first visit, though, was not pleasant. He simply issued a prescription for me and dismissed me. I insisted I wanted to get an injection, because I wanted to stop the pain immediately. After all, I needed to walk my giant dog every day. Reluctantly, he gave the injection to me. I went home and still felt pain, so I took the medication that he prescribed. Still not much improved, I became scared. I could not walk my dog at all. I had to hire my friends to walk my dog. (I am single, so I need to do everything by myself.) I did not follow his advice to rest a lot and thus became exhausted. After one week, my knee got worse. I went to St. Michael's hospital to be diagnosed. They told me that the needle left a blood stain in my membrane. My other knee was painful also, so I let another doctor give me a needle in my knee. After one month, I saw Doctor Wood again, telling him that my knees were killing me—the needles had not worked at all. He changed the medicine and let me go. I took this new medication and had a very good result. After one month, I saw him, and I was very happy. I felt just like a kid. He smiled too. Yet he changed my pills again. He said that my knees had different infections, but he would kill them all. I was very thankful for this.

I did not know his age, but I think that he is as old as my father, since they all enrolled in universities in the same year, 1969. My father was the youngest one in the whole school. Everybody called him 'Little Brother'. Doctors cannot wear rings on their fingers, so I do not know Doctor Wood's marital status. But I do know he is the leader in this hospital surgery clinic. There are, in total, eight doctors. Doctor Wood's favorite task is doing operations, but I am afraid of them. Once he told my family doctor that he wants to do a knee replacement for me, however I refused immediately.

As I like to make friends with all kinds of people, I gave Doctor Wood my books. He was interested in them, saying that, very well, he'd take them. I was encouraged by him and cannot forget this exchange. He suggested that I lose weight so that my knees would carry less weight. I followed his advice and lost weight. When I saw him, I was excited and said: "Doctor Wood, I lose weight." He looked at me and became strict and upset. He said: "it's *lost* weight". I knew that he was teaching me a lesson and wanted me to use the correct tense all the time, especially in my writing. I seldom got so much attention from my parents. They treated me in a different way. *Thank you, Doctor Wood. You not only cured my illness, but also educated me.* I like Doctor Wood's beautiful signature. I cannot sign so elegantly, which is ironic for a writer.

Doctor Wood is strong. He can stand the whole day while treating his patients. I cannot stand even for one hour. I need more exercise. I never see his family pictures in his clinic, so I suppose that he does not want to people to disturb his personal life.

I like Doctor Wood's uniform—it's never too dirty and looks unique.

Today, I have an appointment with Doctor Wood. To be honest, this time, he did not wear his uniform. Instead, he was wearing a Tommy Hilfiger pullover with a lot of dog fur on it. I cannot trust my eyes and now I know that, in my mind, he is unique. (My father sometimes wore a suit with a lot of cat fur on it. His students laughed at him and said to the teacher: "How many dogs did you have? My father smiled and said that he did not have any dogs; he just had two cats.) I love Doctor Wood. He I hope he's keen on me as well.

The Girl I Met

Today I was waiting for Doctor Smith in Four Villages. I saw a baby girl, a toddler, with her mom, who, given her tattered clothes and unkempt appearance, seems to be suffering from a lack of decent income. Poor things. The girl made her way across the carpet. Her movements were a joy to behold—so simple and natural. She is blonde and she loves her mother's partner. Her poses are similar as elegant as a little model. It makes me a bit sad to think that she will possibly be spanked by a parent, and I worry for the dangers she may face in her future. I see her lying on her mother's lap and having fun. She doesn't get punished but instead is consoled. Her mother hasn't done anything wrong. I suggested to her mom that she to Sick Kids Hospital if further health problems should arise. The little girl will be okay in the future, and I highly doubt that the little girl's genetic father has done anything inappropriate. As for now, it looks as if she will need a bit of time to recover, and Sick Kids Hospital would treat her like a princess. The partner, I think, should bring food for the family. The whole family should find social assistance and reunite. I also noticed that these four people wear simple clothes and are quiet, which all arc good signs. The older boy, perhaps, needs to see a psychiatrist, as he is very hyperactive. He is not so well-behaved as the girl. I imagine that their lives have been a nightmare. It is a pity; perhaps they are not from the same father but have the same mother. I highly suggest the mom find a way to survive. It is the only way to support the kids. Otherwise, put them up for adoption.

Kids in this situation are not a worry. Let them learn about animals and religion and tell them what is right and what is wrong. For me, it's that simple.

My New Boyfriend

My friend introduced me to an online dating website. Just two days had passed, and I met two people in person. I like Michael more. He is an entrepreneur who works hard, even on weekends. The first time I met him, we went to Chinatown to eat. He invited me to watch the ballet. I said that I could not understand ballet, but I like strip dancing, which caused him to laugh. Yet suddenly, he said that watching strip dancing was a good idea. He is even a little bit of a sex maniac. He saw me and said that, for his birthday on Thursday, he wanted to invite me to see the strip dancing. I agreed.

On Monday, I bought a lot of Chinese herbs and seafood to cook congee, since he said that he will come to my home. He came late, and by the time he arrived I was very hungry but served him first. Yet he still could not forget about sex and offered this possibility to me. I really did not want to do it, but I am a woman so, I thought, what should I do. I opened YouTube and showed him nude caning videos. He became very excited and eager to whip me immediately. I warned him that my late husband did it to me and if we were married, you couldn't do it too often. We went to the basement guest room, where he and I took off our clothes. I lay on the bed and put a pillow underneath my belly, to raise my butt up more. He whipped me fast and hard. I could not tolerate it. But I did not want to spoil the fun, so I took it. His actions totally shocked me, but I found myself liking it and told him so. I raised my butt more so he can feel more powerful—like a master. He suddenly got up and told me he had an auction to go to tonight. He put on his clothes and left.

I felt sad and just like a mistress. I hated this kind of life. I want to conquer him and my acquaintance.

The Toronto Transit Commission

One day I took the number 77 bus from Runnymede Subway Station. The driver saw a woman who looked like a homeless person. He asked her whether she would like a cup of coffee? She said yes, and he brought two cups of coffee and a muffin. This was not the first time he had bought coffee for her. She took it and did not even say thanks to him. After the bus had been travelling for a bit, the woman decided to get off, asking the driver to give her the muffin too before she departed. The driver gave it to her and asked me: "Do you want a cup of coffee?" I said: "No, thank you." I can only conclude that he is, simply, a good man, through and through, being so kind to people—often strangers to him—in need. I have been very thankful for his kindness over the years and now am proud of him. Once I took Bus 49 and the bus driver give me 25 dollars so I could eat. I thanked him but did not take it. Toronto is just like a big home. I much admire the community-mindedness that I see here. After all, selflessness leads to selfless dedication.

In the morning, I often take the 71 bus at Runnymede Subway Station. The bus driver is very nice and gentle. He was born in Toronto and has a Greek background. He drives safely, but quickly. Also, he always goes to work quite early. Sometimes I have nothing to do, so I wake up and take his bus. He always treats me well. I am very lucky to have a TTC driver friend. He is 62 years old but looks like he is 40 and is over six feet tall—and good looking. I love him. Once I wrote notes to express my love. He told me that he was married, and he has kids that are over 27 years old. He supported his children in finishing their university studies. He is a good father and doesn't wear a wedding ring. Many girls take his bus and I think that they must fall in love with him too. Since he drives the first bus, passengers can easily catch him. I like him very much for this. Now it is the New Year and I buy a card for him. He likes it and says thank you. Compared to his contributions, it was nothing. I hope that these TTC drivers should get rewards from the TTC's head office.

Daddy's Belt

My accountant is my mentor, and I also think of him as a true—even a best—friend. I also call him Daddy. I love him. He helps me with my stocks and edits my essays. He is single, never married, and has no children. I feel just like his kid. He gives me a second childhood, so I call him 'Daddy'.

Today, I let him revise my essays. I have a lot of mistakes, which makes me afraid. I fear that he will be angry. He pulls out his belt and commands: "Pull down your pants." I have no choice but to bare my butt. I stand on the floor and bow towards the bed. He begins to hit me with the belt. At the beginning, I do not feel too much pain and can tolerate it. After a while, I beg him and apologize to him again and again. I am beaten up. He stops and asks me: "Have you studied recently?" I say: "No." He is furious and continues to discipline me. Now I am shaking, and it seems as if I'm returning to my childhood. My parents often beat me hard for no apparent reason. Today, though, since make mistakes, I deserve it. Daddy lets me count the number of beatings, which I peg at over two hundred. He still beats me with the belt, but I do not cry, just shake and apologize. I begin to dodge his belt. He does not blame me. Finally, I count four hundred times; he stops. I say: "Thank you, Daddy. I won't let you down again. Please forgive me." He sits down and ties the belt.

He tells me that my butt is bruised and swelling, but of course I cannot see it. He uses the cell phone to take photos. It is all black and blue. He lets me sit down and teaches me how to correct the mistakes. I cannot sit down directly, instead sitting down on my both hands. My mentor does not sympathize with me, but instead only teaches me how to correct the mistakes, one by one. In some places,

I do not understand why I've made errors. I am afraid. He does not punish me again. He says: "Next time, you ask me again." Suddenly, I feel released.

Daddy loves me. I know it. I published some books, yet the sales volumes are not good. He wants me to have a leap in the quality of my new books. I should try my best to reach his goals. Today he uses the traditional method to educate me. I should blame myself. Daddy's left arm was broken once. He does not want to damage it again. I swear that I will not waste my time and, instead, vow to improve the quality of my writing. *Daddy I am sorry…*

Dates

Recently, I put five adverts, looking for personal company, even a relationship, in the Toronto Star newspaper. I also joined an online dating website. Since then, many people have replied to me, and I am overwhelmed by their flattery.

One man, Dan, told me that he was a dog walker, and his income was very good, over two hundred bucks every day. He wrote that he loved his job, and that he had two dogs. The first time we met together, he was, let's just say, very active. He introduced himself and took off his clothes and talked nicely to me, and he lived not far from me, just a twelve-minute drive.

In fact, he lives in a condominium. He let me touch his cock and even ejaculated. In the early morning, he rushed to leave, claiming he had to walk the dog. After one week, online saw him again online. We were both excited. He joked that he wanted to whip me with a wet noodle. He took off his underwear and faced me, beginning to satisfy himself. Before long, he ejaculated. Later, we talked about many things. Both of us were happy. He graduated from the University of Western Ontario with a bachelor's degree. After three weeks, we encountered each other online again. I was eager to chat with him. He was absent-minded. He said: "I am one of the million people watching the Super Bowl." I was upset and said: "I am the Bowl. Do you want to go to my home tonight? I am horny." He did not want to be interrupted and kept silent. When the game finished, he texted me: "Perhaps you can masturbate to quell your need." Then he said that he needed to walk his dogs, shower, and go to bed…" I knew that I had been so wrong. I felt lonesome and humiliated. Hurt, I typed: "Why did you slap me?" A rather pointed question, but at that time, I needed to be direct. Dan's reactions had hurt me and forced me to try to find my self-respect. He did not answer for a while. In his mind, he had taught me a lesson. He typed: "What are you talking about? I never did that. Nor would I ever!" He was the first man I met in person from an online dating website.

Yesterday, one man called me. He said that he had read my advertisement in the Toronto Star. I met him for the first time at my home. When he introduced himself, I did not see too many outstanding features on him. He might have felt that and known that I was not much interested in him. He said goodbye, and as I stood up, he suddenly hugged me. He held me and kissed me, even putting his one hand in my pants and touching my clitoris and pussy. I was shocked. He did not hurt me but made me feel very comfortable. After a while, he asked me if we could have more intimacy or not. I said yes to more. We went to basement, my guest room. We were both naked. He continued to touch my sexual organs. I felt like the experience was out of this world. In fact, I had never been so excited. After five minutes, I began to bleed. He said that he could not make love with me since I was bleeding and put on his clothes and left. I found some pads. My womb was felt very painful. It was strange—he had not made love to me, and his love touch had been very gentle. Why had I begun to bleed?

At night, I still felt excited, yet pained. Strangely, I was happy for that; it was just like the feeling imagined one would have during pregnancy. My bleeding lasted a couple of days. I knew that I had met an expert at sex.

Crisis

Today I woke up very early. I took the bus just for fun. Suddenly, I recalled that yesterday I had seen a blind guy beating his guide dog, which was a German Sheppard. I felt furious and stopped him, prompting him to almost beat me. I felt sorry for his guide dog, because I had met it once and I had given him a shawarma wrap, which he had liked and had wanted to eat. The blind guy, though, had forced him to go away. As I wanted to help the dog, this made me very sad. In the meantime, the bus had passed the Toronto Police 12 Division, and I had gotten off and walked into the police division. I told them what I'd seen and showed the photos of both the man and the dog, full of hope that they could rescue the creature.

Maybe my words were too strong and hard to accept. Maybe my body language was not good. They asked me what I would do after that. I said that I would see my psychiatrist at noon. The police officer I was speaking to directed two other policemen to drive me to my doctor's office. One policeman was a nurse, the other was a crisis intervention specialist. I still felt sorry for the dog because I hadn't rescued him from the devil. On the road, I talked to the nurse policeman to him, saying that I was okay and explaining why I had come to the police station. He was frank and sometimes even joked with me. The other policeman often watched me through the mirror.

Soon they dropped me off at the psychiatrist's office. I got off and said thank you to them. I saw the doctor and told him what had happened. He did not blame me and treated me very kindly. Now I know that the crisis had passed. I thanked the police and my doctor for helping me at the time. I hoped that they could help the dog too.

Father Ted

When I first came to Canada, I lived near the intersection of King Street and Jameson Avenue, where a large Catholic Church stands. The church has a food bank. As it was hard to find a stable job and I needed a lot of time to study, I visited the food bank. Father Ted oversaw the food bank. He stood about 1.68 meters tall, had blue eyes and brown hair. He was kind and strictly followed the rules. At the beginning, I just got my food and went home. Then the food bank was recruiting so became a volunteer. Why did I do it? Because volunteers could get more food. Father Ted let me separate the food for months. Then, noticing that I didn't have any problems communicating in English, he allowed me to call out the people's names so they could get their food. I studied French for two years. I could announce their names even though I had never seen them before, but I sometimes mispronounced their names. The people were not happy and yelled at me and said that I should go back to school. I also felt ashamed. Father Ted never blamed me for that. He knew that I tried my best. This sudden criticism tricked me into deciding to go back to school. Finally, I was admitted to Brock University as a Master of Education Major. Now that I recall it, I still needed to thank Father Ted.

When I worked in the food bank, I found that one door was never locked. There was a refrigerator in it and in the refrigerator, there were birthday cakes every week. I did the volunteer job and, at the same time, enjoyed eating the cakes. It was very fresh, although it was leftover cake. (Now, you know my favorite food is birthday cake—I love it.) After eating cake, I did not feel hungry anymore. The most important thing was that I did not need money to buy something that was expensive—I could not have afforded it. I ate it for free for over two months. One day a volunteer came into the room in which I was eating. He saw me and wanted to go out. I stopped him and told him that he could eat the cake also, but he refused. Soon, Father Ted came in. He asked me whether I had eaten those cakes or not. I said yes. He was very angry and told me the cakes were for the church's poor families to eat, not for the food bank clients to eat. He blamed me for this transgression—and I knew that I had been wrong. I did not say anything; I just lowered my head. But this had happened when I had first come to Canada, and I was, at the same time, thankful that the cakes had, in a way, saved my life and helped me get through the hardest time in my life. Until now, I still thank Father Ted for not firing me from my volunteer job. He treated me fairly and nicely. For this, I love him.

In the Western world, Christmas is the biggest festival of the whole year. When I first came to Canada, I was alone and had no idea even what kind of food people ate at Christmas. I remembered the hymn 'Silent Night', though. So, I did my best to fit in. I held my camera, walked outside people's houses and took photos of their lovely Christmas decorations. Sometimes I watched them through the windows. Their homes looked so quaint and lovely, and I felt as if I could almost *see* the love emanating between the inhabitants. I saw ham, turkey, cake…whole families enjoying Christmas together. My bare feet were in wet shoes in the snow, outside people's houses. I did not cry; I just felt lonely. I suddenly remembered that the church would have Mass. I could at least find some company there, so I went to church. Father Ted held the Mass. I came in and kneeled, lowering my head in reverence. At this moment, I really wanted to kiss his hand and call him Father. It seemed that I had a big home. I am not alone anymore. After Mass, Father Ted walked up to me. He told me that tomorrow Christmas Day we had a dinner; I was welcome to attend. I watched him; he might not know his little effort for me a new immigrant meant what. I said goodbye to Father Ted. On Christmas day, I went to Chinatown to buy dumpling wraps, and ground pork and vegetables. I went home to make Chinese dumplings. At the church dinner everybody needed to bring one dish. I was not an exception. At 5pm, I brought my dish to the church's diner. I could not be happier, when I chatted and learnt from the Bible. That was my first Christmas in Canada. Father Ted wore black clothes. He was also happy about our contributions.

Since then, twenty-one years have passed. One day, I passed by the church. I came in. I did not see Father Ted. I asked church clerk, he went to other places for a few days, but was not sure about the exact day he would come back. I was a little bit disappointed. I donated 5 dollars in the box and went home. I already did not live there. It is not convenient to go to that church. God bless Father Ted who still in that church and still energetic. I never dare to forget his lessons and favours. He is forever in my heart. God bless him.

Bo Comes Back

Bo is my tenant's cat, who has a long pure black fur. I love him. He is also my cat Prince's good company.

Last year November, my tenant moved out. Bo also went with his owner. I missed him a lot. I thought that I would not see him again. Hence, I adopted a new kitty named Milo. He became a companion for Prince my ten years old beloved cat. Yet, Milo is a big bully and extremely naughty. He beats Prince all the time and eats Prince's treats and cat food. I am really upset.

In January this year, my old tenant wanted to move back. I was full of promises. Soon in March 2023, Bo jumped into my sight. I am very happy. I told Bo's owner that I wanted Bo to help Prince beat Milo. Bo is very timid. He did not go to the first floor and the second floor for a week. The worst thing is Milo often goes to basement to bully Bo. My dream has shut down. Bo still has beautiful long shining and smart fur. He always has a sense of superiority. I love him just like a mom. One and half years ago, Bo just came to my home; I taught him to call me mama. He knew it and called me mama. Prince and Milo, all can call me mama. I love all my babies no matter what.

Bo loves his owner and always follows him just like a doggie. Every day when his owner comes home, he will run and be welcome him. I really admire their relationship. My kitties watch me come and go; that's it. My kitties eat *blue buffalo wild* cat food, which is the most expensive cat food in the pet store. Yet, they sometimes steal Bo's food. I feel very angry and sorry. Bo never eats my kitties' food and even when I give him my cats' treats; he does not eat it either. What a good, adorable creature he is.

Bo came back. My mother's love is full of him. I often say: "Love me love my cat." I like his owner too. He is just like my younger brother. I love Bo forever.

Beresford Avenue Yard Sale

Today I woke up early and went to Freshco, the local grocery store. My neighbour couple were busy preparing for a yard sale. I was very excited and promised to buy something from them. The wife said that today is the Beresford Avenue yard sale.

I finished shopping in Freshco and rushed to our street yard sale. I bought a lamp and books from my neighbour. Then I went to a lady's front yard. I found a stuffed rabbit doll; she said that it was free. I got it with a smile. I said thank you and went to another house. I saw a cookbook I liked. I just wanted to know the price. I saw a note that everything is free. I was very happy and took the recipe book and spicy jars in the bags. I continued to go. One family was selling chairs, which were big and very comfortable. I asked how much they were. She said free. I could not believe it. I gave the husband two dollars and let him bring the chair to my home porch since my legs were very painful. They accepted. I went to a family. They sell pocket alcohol containers. I bought two for my tenant, who works outside for high-rise building window cleaning. He often feels cold. I also bought one box chopsticks and racks, one box plates and more books. I let the kids send them to my home. I saw a family selling community reward ornaments I was hurrying to get it. I fell down on the pavement. An EMS lady and a gentleman helped me get up. I asked how much were the community reward ornaments? She said it was free. I took one. I was very happy and sad too. I really wanted to get my own reward by myself.

Finally I went to a store's back yard. All kinds of things were on sale. I brought a macaw or say parrot oil painting for five dollars and a garden rooster, whose original price was 89 dollars. I bought it for ten dollars. I bought a large set of silver utensils for 30 dollars, two cushions for 30 dollars, one rabbit ratio drawings for 25 dollars, rabbit plates, boxes and bowls for 35 dollars I love them. I cannot carry them home. I called a taxi and came home.

When I went home. I found that the family selling the chairs brought two chairs on my veranda. I appreciated it. In the afternoon, the couple passed by my house. I gave them five dollars for the chairs. They refused. They said that they would like to give them to me.

My neighbour had a lot of books. I found some again and bought them. I also bought a baby hat, and some fluffy animals, that I liked. My neighbour wanted to donate something. I found a bathing cloth for me and a cowboy scarf which was for my dog Buddy. My neighbour had a much better life than me. I want to thank my street neighbours. I love our street.

Campaign US President Joe Biden

If anyone thinks President Joe Biden spends more money than he deserves, she or he is totally wrong. Because they do not know how he saves the USA more than ever. President Joe Biden opened a new page in the relationship with southern pacific countries. I feel strange why many people are still against him. President Joe Biden is a foodie. He tastes all kinds of food from majority countries. President Joe Biden is an animal lover. He especially loves dogs. His favorite dog Champ helped his campaign a lot.

First lady Jill Biden is independent and intelligent. She not only supports her husband but also works on her own careers. She published books and articles. Jill Biden is the First Lady who was Second Lady in US history. I love Jill Biden too. She is kind and beautiful. She loves her stepchildren and her own children at the same time. She is one of the best mothers I ever knew. She also loves dogs and cats. I like it. Jill Biden works in the education field and keeps her financial independence. She is a perfect example for modern women.

Some people blame the Biden government which did not fix the low employment rates. In my opinion the low employment rate is not one country's problem. It is a global phenomenon. The Biden government did a better job than most other countries. I appreciate him. He is a good decision maker. President Joe Biden cares about the grass roots. He passed the students' relief debts policy and helped lower income families lowing the cost. President Joe Biden protects marginalized people. For example, he voices his concern for LGBTQ people and homeless persons. He understands and sympathizes with the American people more than most politicians. He is very strategic and diplomatic. He has empathy, a character trait that seems to be increasingly lacking in some popular politicians late to the rodeo—such as the convicted felon and megalomaniac running for president south of the border. President Joe Biden, on the other hand, is a gentleman with a gold heart.

King's Noodle Restaurant

Today is Saturday December 9th, 2023. I ordered a roast pork at King's Noodle Restaurant one week ago. It is located at the Dundas Street West and Spadina Avenue intersection. I often go to this restaurant for BBQ ducks. It is very delicious and famous in the whole Chinatown. Sometimes I buy roast pork feet, because it is cheaper. I do not know which parts are a better taste for the whole toast pork.

For our church's Christmas party, I told our bishop that I will contribute a roast pork since this year I have not paid tithing. He said: "thank you." I went to King's Noodle Restaurant to book a roast pork. The deposit is 150 dollars, and the total price is about 300, which is the same as other restaurants. I told them to please give me a bigger one since our church have almost 200 members. They readily promised me.

December 9th, 2023, at 4 pm, my friend who is also active member of our church drove me to pick up the pork. The church is near the restaurant 14 minutes to drive there. I paid $150. They help me put the pork in the car. They do not offer cutting pork. The smells are very good. Soon we came back to the church. A gentleman who is one of our church members helped me bring the pork in the dining hall. The man who drove me to the restaurant knew how to cut the whole pork. He used a knife and fork to cut it.

He is very happy, because he said that the whole roast pork is well done and very delicious. He tasted a little bit since his wife did not permit him to eat meats. He told me that he learned cutting pork when he was young. At that time, his father brought him to the mountains to hunt wild boars.

At 6:30 pm, our dinner began. One church member also brought a roast pork. He cut the pork in a stranger way. Anyway, our members and guests ate up too.

My roast pork is very popular. Everyone picks it. The guy who brought a pork used long cutting knives to serve us. Even for second helpings people who want the meat can have it. It is amazing, I got a third helping. All the people eating the pork said that it was delicious and wanted me to order it next year. I promised that I will.

I wrote this essay to thank to King's Noodle Restaurant's staff, who serve their customers so nice. As a regular customer I will come there more often.

Fingerprint

Someone said that my books are like fingerprints unique. Firstly, I must say that in the whole world, we do have several people who do not have fingerprints on their fingers. Secondly, everybody is unique. Our experiences are different, although the history always repeats again and again. Literature is for all the people. We can write our memories, which are amazing and brilliant! My personal rules: write what really happened. Then write some things that are deeply in your minds. Please do not read other people's books. You are your own keepers; we do not need others to lead. The University of Toronto Dental School

In my mind, the University of Toronto Dental School is one of the best dental departments in all of Canada. However, when I became their patient, I knew that I had been totally wrong in choosing them.

My teeth had often ached. I went to see many dentists, but still, they did not solve my problems. My friend introduced me to the University of Toronto's dental school so that I could consult with one of their dentists. Happy about this, I felt it was a great idea and so, on a humid Monday morning, I went there. First, I had to register. This was easy: They checked my history of illnesses very carefully, then made some appointments for me. For virtually every appointment, I noticed that would need to wait for two to three weeks, or more. It was for teaching purposes, I was told students must be there, on the spot, with the teachers informing them how to execute each procedure. Things seem to be taking a bad turn for me. For my first wisdom tooth problem, I had to visit them three times, before the dentist-student was finally removed by teacher, since the young female student was not able to find the strength to pull it out. It was okay, as, in the end, the teacher successfully pulled it out. Whew! I had eliminated one big burden.

Then, they found that one of my upper teeth needed root canal treatment. I was pointed in the direction of another female student. I wanted to change doctors. One male teacher, who was double D (doctoral degree and dentist), told me if I wanted him to do it, he needed to treat everybody. Discouraged, I gave up. That female student allowed me to go home to wait, but after one month, I still did not have word on my status. I called her, and she said that I simply had too many illnesses. She needed to find the proper authority to determine if she do the procedure or not. Before this time, I had already taken many X-rays for my teeth and paid both the X-ray fee as well as the examination fees, which were several hundred dollars. My tooth was of no use anymore. I felt very uncomfortable, and another month passed. I finally decided to quit this U of T clinic, and, instead, went to a Chinese dental clinic. The dentist there told me that it was not necessary to keep the problematic tooth. He suggested that they remove it. I agreed, and, with my tooth soon extracted, had finally finished my teeth troubles.

During my visit to U of T's dental school, I had found that the students always chatted with each other. They did not study hard or help patients. They were more lacking in professional knowledge and in spirit of dedication than the private dentists.

The University of Toronto is one if the best universities in Canada, even in the whole world. I have admired it ever since I first arrived in Canada. Maybe now, though, it is time for its dental department to walk down the altar.

My Beloved Husband

My late husband was a good joke teller. He often said some jokes to the people around him. Once he told me two fries and the shit' joke, I laughed a lot. He also told me something is funny, for example: in his factory, there was an engineer whose name was Danny. His skills were not too great. My husband once sang to him, "oh, Danny boy the pipes pipes are calling …". The engineer was very angry.

Since he liked to tell jokes to people, they also liked to fool him. Once he went to hospital for his back pain, the doctor saw his name and asked him what kind of job he did. He said security. The doctor said that: "Hi you are really Dennis Miners." Our surname is pronounced "sub junk" we all told people our name pronounced "subject". We did not like people calling us "sub junk" either.

Dennis had a good friend who taught him how to do leather work. In our home, we have a lot leather tools and all kinds of stamps. Some are very rare. His father even made some unique tools for him to make leather work. Unfortunately, his friend passed away. He had not done leather work for years.

My late husband was very kind. One of his neighbours often borrowed money from Dennis. He did not like it, yet he lent it to him. This neighbour call Dennis "an angel" sometimes, he never returned the money. Dennis lent 5000 dollars to his factory's woman worker in 1990s. She did not return even a cent.

Dennis could dance Ukrainian traditional folk dance well. When he was young, his parents sent him to Ukrainian dancing school to study. He sometimes danced for me. I love it so much.

Dennis loved cats. He did not like dogs. He went to the humane society to adopted Harry a male tabby cat. Harry was just tried to be put down, because he was very aggressive and attacked humans. Dennis could not see a cat being killed.

He immediately adopted Harry and brought him to the vet Saini. Vet Saini did the examination of Harry. He was in good shape. He neutered Harry. Dennis brought Harry home and was very happy. Harry clawed Dennis's legs causing bleeding. Everybody saw Dennis's legs. They all wanted him to give up Harry. He refused to do so. He loves Harry just like his elder son. After half a year, Harry did not claw Dennis too much anymore. Harry died when he was 19 years old.

Dennis liked music. As a reward, I often played Chinses classic songs to him. He did not understand Chinese, yet he liked the tunes. I was very glad to provide Chinese culture to him.

My late husband was very kind to me and others. Before I married with my late husband, my nose was bleeding when I ate food. After we were married, we ate in the restaurants, and I cooked delicious food. My nose never bled anymore. When I am eating, just a little bit snot discharges. I appreciate him forever. He saved my life. I love him forever.

Nina and Q

Another night I am on the TTC bus. I met Nina and her beloved fur ball son Q, who is a husky and German shepherd mix male doggie. Q is one of my favorite dogs. He has two tufts of fair-coloured fur surrounding both eyes, so people call him a four-eyed dog. Q has black fur from head to tail. His belly and butt are all golden fur, which is very beautiful. I love it. I just get on a streetcar. There is a loud quarrel sound in my ears. I do not know why I just heard one girl yelling to the other girl that she smells and needs a shower. The other girl fought back and said that girl is a sex worker. She wore a skirt, even though it was winter in Toronto. She was not the smartest, I though. I saw the doggie and played with him. I asked the owner his name. She said it was Q. She told me her name is Nina. I was glad that I met two new friends now, who I could grow to love, I felt. Nina bought several burgers in McDonald's. She just ate the bread and left the whole meat for Q. She bought two donuts. She ate one; Q had the other. I gave Q a box of fried peanuts, which he ate up

I noticed that Nina often falls asleep. She has one small luggage and one big bag of beer bottles. Carefully, I asked her why she hadn't found a place to live. She said that she had lost her job as a cleaner last July. Now, she cannot pay the bills and rent. She became homeless. The government cut half of her income, which was reduced to 385 dollars. Often, she just wanders the streets. She told me there were some clothes and some drinks in her luggage. If she sees some beer bottles, she will pick up and get some change for the TTC bus fare. I cannot let her live in my house, because I have four cats in the house. Q is two years old and has not been neutered. They will fight together. Now it is 8 o'clock in the morning. I call my friend. She has a house. I tell her about my friend with a dog. It is okay to live in your basement. At the beginning, she hesitates. I persuade her. She agreed. Nina is a black girl and was born in Toronto. Her parents went back to Trinidad and Tobago. She is 31 years old. She deserves a better life. My friend sent an email to Nina, then Nina sent it to her worker. She is very happy, as am I—I've managed to cheer her up somewhat.

Nina lost her home over half a year. Her situation is now very bad. Her ankles have swollen. She cannot fit into regular shoes. She wears a pair of sandals in winter. She tells me she needs to go to washroom to pee every two or three hours. Yet I never see her drinking water. She often uses a cup to feed Q water and doggie can food. She cannot carry dog dry food as it is too heavy and needs space. Q loves canned food. It takes one bite to finish. I even laugh at Q. Now Q is also tired. Sometimes he sleeps on seats or on the floor of street cars. I feel sad and happy for Q. I suggest that Nina applies for ODSP (Ontario Disability Support Program). She is accepted. Nina with Q beg often, because they need to survive. They need food. Nina tried many times to find a job. Yet she has no home, no car, and with a fur baby Q. what can she do. I do not blame Nina. That is why I persuaded her to apply for ODSP.

She has no family doctor. Her family doctor is retired. My online search found one walking in clinic near my home. Yet she cannot find her health card. We go to Service Ontario to apply for one. She is very happy.

It is noon now. Nina is very hungry, but Q is still excited and pees every one or two minutes. He really needs a girlfriend now, desperately. I ask her what kind of food she likes most. She said Caribbean food, Chinese food or fast food. We go to a Caribbean restaurant near my home to buy two boxes of curry goat with rice and red beans. I Paid 34 dollars. My pleasure. We go to my home. Q first rushed into the living room. Immediately, my cats ran as fast as possible and make huge noise. The tenant cat directly runs into basement; the other cats run into my upstairs room. Q still does not feel satisfied. He chases them up and down. Finally, Nina pulls him back in the kitchen and ties his leash on the door handle. We eat goat and rice. Q does not steal, instead is busy seeing my backyard though the big kitchen window. I joke about him; the big window is Q's TV. Nina is cold. I make tea for her. I ask her Q eat sanding or not. She said yes, he eats sanding. I open a big can of food, which he eats reluctantly. Then, Nina and Q are both tired. They sleep until 1 pm. I call Nina. She cannot wake up. I see Q close his eyes and not move. Finally at 1: 10 pm, I wake them up, because Nina has a walking in doctor's appointment at 1:40 pm. I walk them to the bus stop and say goodbye to them. We leave phone numbers for each other and promise to be good friends forever. I also give Q three big jars of peanut butter, hopefully he likes it. When I go home, I still miss them. I feel that today I didn't waste my time. I help a person in need. She may change her life after today. She finds a home to live with her handsome doggie Q. She is pretty, too.

Sometimes readers said that I wrote white people's literature. I do not deny it. But from now on, I am a writer to portrait all nations. We need fair play.

One Night's True Adventure

It is 5pm, and Nina called me. She had something on her plate. Could be good, I thought. We decided to see each other. We met at Keele subway station at 6:30 pm. I was very excited, because I was seeing my two friends, Nina and Q. I said that, at Yonge and Dundas Square there's a Popeye's Chicken fast food restaurant. It is the best Popeye's chicken chain restaurant in the whole of Toronto, I'll treat you there. So we went to the restaurant, where I bought three Tuesday combos, two for Nina and one for me. I also brought three doggie canned food to Q. Q likes them.

After we ate, Nina suggested that we go to Union Station for free cell phone charging. We sit in waiting area and face the Tim Horton. I play with Q. He is all wet and has no clothes on. Nina says that the clothes are dirty and too long. About 12 am, Nina guides us to Go Train to a small city near Hamilton. I never take the Go Train, so I am extremely excited. Although it is midnight, I am still curious enough to look out the window. Q sits facing me. I play with his fur and pat him often. I love him very much. Soon we pass Mississauga, Oakville, Burlington, and some small cities surrounding lake shore Ontario Canada. Then we get off the train. We cross a bridge and then walk to the street. I saw some houses not in the good shape. I do not know even the city's name. Nina walks very fast. I can hardly catch up. I see a few homeless people sleep outside the church or on the street. The rain does not stop yet. Q runs here and there. No one holds the leash. He is very happy, and I call to him; he stops to wait for me, peeing to mark the roads. Nina still walks very fast. I guess the chicken I gave her must be helping her energy level. I am out of breath, but she doesn't seem to care. It is 1:40 am, I am afraid and feel death passing me. *Nina worked as a cleaner. If she has some bad friends, I may die here. I really do not know anything about where I am.* I feel extremely tired, since I am carrying a lot of drinks. I suddenly see McMaster University, and across the street is the Hamilton City Hall. I guess that it is Hamilton's downtown. Crisis averted.

We continue to go. Q sees me struggling, and poops in the intersection while waiting for me. I know that I'm appreciated and think that it is indeed true, dog is man's best friend. Soon I am out of breath again. This time I do not follow her so closely. I've already decided that if I cannot find her, I'll call 911. Eventually, I catch her, and she says to me that soon we will go to the Hamilton Go Bus Station. To my surprise, the door of the Go Bus Station is the middle of a concrete bridge. I did not even dream about it. Suddenly, I regret that I have trusted someone too soon—after all, I'm following someone I barely know to some strange new places at midnight. Now I know why people go missing or get murdered. Alas, I am almost there.

The Go Bus comes. I pay and sit behind Q. Nina falls asleep. I pet Q and look out the window, the rich green and brown kaleidoscope of urban Ontario passing by. I see a Tim Hortons and I take comfort in knowing that I am still in Canada and near Toronto. The bus journey takes about one hour. We get to Richmond Hill, where we wait over one hour to catch the bus to Toronto's Finch Go Bus and Finch TTC Station. Now I feel safe. I realize I have been wrong—I should not be so easily seeking to satisfy my curiosity and putting myself in danger. I love dogs, but human beings are much more dangerous. Note this adventure for future reference.

51 Division M Hayford

M Hayford is a rotten apple. He works at Toronto Police 51 Division. Under his protection are many neighbourhood businesses, and he's also a regular patron. Of course, being a police officer, he does not pay for food and drink. His rule is: not having to pay is the best cost. He often hangs out at Popeye's Chicken fast food restaurant at Yonge and Dundas Square for lunch and supper. For him, it's not a big deal. He even collects his protection fees from them.

On this day, he gets a call against Popeye's. He knows it's time to get even. He drives a police car and calls two other policemen to also go there. He understands that he is due his under the table money. His other rule: no money, no peace.

M Hayford is a sergeant. He is trying his best to become a staff sergeant but has failed. His sergeant's title, in fact, has only been conferred on him because he has served in the force for over twenty years. His colleagues say that if he had not exploited public office for private gain, he would already be staff sergeant.

Before long, he arrives at the restaurant. A woman has called the police and he asks the cashier what has happened. The cashier notices him and smiles then talks differently. Next, Hayford sternly asks the woman to leave immediately. She feels slighted, humiliated, and violated. Finding her inner strength, she does not leave and, in fact, requests to see the store's owner. Hayford and the accompanying two officers respond by handcuffing her and pushing her out, handing her a 75-dollar fine for trespassing.

I remember one and half years ago, I was listening to my inner voice, which very much helped me. After all, don't we all take advice from our subconscious from time to time? I considered how I could reward them. The answer was that they were in Police 51 Division. I went home and got 500 dollars, which I took to this division. I wrote letters of thanks to Warden and Smith, who I imagined were advocating for me. Two weeks later, I called the police station. They said that they never received the money and letters, which made me feel very angry. I reported online to Toronto Police headquarters, who immediately started an investigation. This division is police detective Murdoch's division. Now, to my mind, it is nothing but a garbage bin. I write this essay to warn people away from these tricksters.

Banknote 2

The Banknote, near Annette Street and Jane Street, is very popular now. People come to the store to buy or sell coins or some other precious things. The store's owner has a good reputation. Everyone likes him. Occasionally, he gets some counterfeit coins or fake antiques, which he keeps for himself and never sells, not wanting to pollute the market with such junk. I am grateful for his moral character.

Now he deals with big or small treats every day, earning good money, thank you very much. In fact, he is quite rich now. Sometimes, he becomes especially attached to some coins, which he keeps in his collection. He said that his descendants may like them too.

I as a regular customer, I never bargain with him, but he often gives me discounted prices. I am much moved by his generosity. He once had a dream that he let everyone have their own coin. So, he does not raise his prices when people really like a specific coin. This is why I trust him and admire him.

The owner is also the President of The Ontario Coin Society, and is very much deserving of this title. His father knowing his son is a good businessman, helps him out—especially with deal-making. His sincerity and generosity, in my view, are the qualities that make him so successful.

My Home

My home is my sweet nest. One day, though, my beloved husband passed away. This made me feel bitter. But eight years have passed. I have tenants, yet I do not know why I rented to four Nigerian people. Only one of them is okay.

The first Nigerian tenant said that he was an international student. He was shorter than me. On his body, there are a lot of scars. It looked like he is a soldier who had just come back from the front. He smoked cannabis every day and had a bad temper. He was not good at cooking and often threw out a lot of food. He did not put the old food in the green bin. Instead, he was stuffing it in the sink. Finally, I had to find a plumber to fix the backup. My tenant paid 100 dollars of the total cost, and I paid 20 dollars. He also damaged my burner. This time, I took the hit myself (which came to 80 dollars), not wanting to bother him (besides, he had he already delayed paying the rent).

Since that time, I made an important discovery about my client. Taking the TTC bus, I found that he had been going to the factory instead of to school. He has a turtle as his pet, but he did not treat it nicely. The turtle was suffering, sitting directly under the light bulb all the time, and the food he was feeding it was disgusting. The worse thing was that the tank water stunk. He put a lot of water in the tank. The turtle was forced to swim all the time. I really felt pity for it. Fortunately, when he moved out, he left the turtle to me. I immediately threw out the old turtle food, buying good food for it. Some of its food cost me 25 dollars, yet that was my pleasure.

What's more, this tenant stole my cat Milo's four leader collars and name tags, which cost me over 100 dollars. The police came to my home and found one collar with a name tag in his room. I don't know why, but this one collar with a name tag, which I put in the drawer, was also lost.

The second Nigeria guy almost moved in at the same time as the first one. He also claimed that he was an international student. He was 47 years old and wanted to study at Seneca College, but he failed the test and soon moved out. He took one or two showers every day. I did not know what he was doing in there. Every shower took over one hour. I just have one bathroom on the second floor. Sometimes, I had to use the washroom so badly I was in pain holding back. Now, thankfully, he has also flown the coop—once again, Lady Luck strikes!

The third one, though, is a very good Nigerian. He lived in my home for over one month. Yet his social worker did not issue to him the 650 dollars monthly rent he had to pay me. *Bye-bye*. He gave me 200 dollars for breaking the lease—a small consolation, but I'll take it. He is a Black Muslim and was very polite. I liked him.

The fourth one, on the other hand, was the worst. She was a black, very bossy, and rude. She sometimes wanted to clean my house, but she damaged it. I told her very politely not to clean my home. (I have a cleaner who comes every month.) Still, she did not listen. All my toilet paper, kitchen supplies, and napkins were soon used up. She even threw away my kitchen towels and stole my refrigerator stickers. I lost all kinds of things, which were not cheap to replace. She lifted my food, for crying out loud.

What's more, she liked to search through my cabinets and table drawers, stealing something that had been in them. The worst thing, though, was that she beat me up. Once, I told her, since she had moved into my house over 12 days earlier, she had never paid rent or her deposit. *Please move out*. She was furious and smashed and kicked my door. She blocked people from seeing her room. She said that she would not move out or pay me the rent. This led to blows being exchanged. She swore at me and smashed my microwave door and damaged it. I felt very angry and pushed her. She responded by grabbing a steel water bottle full of water and beating me multiple times, bruising my arm and back. I called the police, who told me to go to the landlord and tenant board to solve the problem. They asked me to call the EMS, which I readily did. The EMS arrived and examined my bruise, blood pressure, blood sugar and EGG. They were okay, and only my blood sugar was high (12.9). *What a relief!* After they left, though, the tenant continued to swear at me and smashed my door. She opened the window and outside door, claiming to want fresh air, but it was 15 degrees below zero out there. What could I do? Fight with her? I just could stay on the first floor to protect my property. She swore at me the whole day and whole night. Desperate, I called my lawyer and he said that he would help me. He immediately sent letters to her which informed her of her highly illegal (not to mention downright scary) behaviour. She had sworn loudly at us, and my other tenants felt that she could not be tolerated.

Tuesday my accountant and I bought KFC to eat in my home. We talked and ate for over one hour. Then he helped me put my waste bin and take the recycling bin out. Hearing him going out, she went into the kitchen to swear at me again and splashed water and dish soap all over the place. I asked kindly to not use my dish soap in such a way but, in her anger, she pushed me. Offended by this act of raw aggression, I pushed her back. But this was clearly not the woman's first rodeo. She immediately grabbed my plastic ladle and beat me multiple times across my head: my cheek was swollen; my head was bleeding. She finally beat me very hard, even breaking the ladle. Finally, she stopped. She had hit me so fast I did not have the ability to react quickly enough to protect myself. Feeling blood trickling down my face, I immediately called the police and EMS. The tenant swearing so loudly at me that my voice could not be heard by the operator. Finally, knowing my address, the latter sent the ambulance to me. Not only was the left side of my face completely covered in blood, but my shirt was also blood-soaked. The EMS worker was the consummate professional—they expertly cleaned and bandaged my wounds. When the police came, they found my bag and coat and asked me some questions but said that they couldn't immediately arrest her as she was in the shower and only after that would they bring her to the police station. Soon after, EMS drove me to the hospital, where a doctor cleaned the wound and applied four staples to my head. Thankfully, they gave me a taxi slip for my return home, as I was feeling as dizzy as a boxer at the end of a prize fight.

The result of this experience was that I had an aversion to renting my house to anyone who had lived between Lagos and Abuja in the future. Good luck to all the landlords.

Anthony Fahy

If ever one is feels as if they are lacking colour in your life, the antidote to this absence may be a simple one: get a tenant. Fahy was my first tenant. I rented a room beginning November 5th, 2021. When he first moved in, I was excited, because my late husband had passed away over six years earlier. I was very lonely and had become sick twice.

Fahy was a thin man, a physical trait which must have served him well in his skateboarding riding. The young man was a master at it. To me, he looked very funny, with his fluffy hair and a constantly bemused look on his face. An animal lover, he came complete with a black cat, whom he called Bo. He casually told me that it was female, yet a closer examination revealed that Bo was, in fact, a boy who had only one testicle. Today, Bo has become our belt of love. We all love Bo and take care of him. Of course, I have Prince, the black cat I mentioned earlier, and Fahy likes him too. Fahy never closes his bedroom door because of Bo.

In the beginning, though, I did not lock the door either because of my other cat, the hyperactive Prince. Now, despite this kaleidoscope of personalities, we are all good companions. Sometimes I go to Fahy's room and take photos of Bo. I look at his treasures, but I am careful not to touch them. In turn, he is free to borrow from my coin collection. Our relationship is blossoming into a friendship of sorts.

Fahy is a chef, spending his nights slaving away in the heat of the kitchen at Toronto famous old Drake hotel. I have never tasted his food, but not for lake of trying—he simply refuses to cook here in the home. Perhaps I will one day tie him up in the kitchen and point a gun at him while ordering to cook at my command. That'll get the job done.

In my mind, he is like a younger brother, and because of this, I am willing to yield to him. For instance, I remember that when I first install home monitors, I was careful to install them both in my room as well as in his. In this way, I could ensure that my tenants' actions were all on the up-and-up by viewing any activities on my cell phone. One day shortly after the installation, I observed Bo on his bed and called to him. It felt weird as Bo glanced up at the camera, ostensibly looking directly at me. Fahy was astounded by this security feature; nevertheless, appeared to happily go about his business under the watchful eye of the camera.

Soon, however, I found that the monitor had become dark and, in a bit of a panic, called the technician to come and have a look at it. The cause of the problem soon became apparent: Fahy had put black tape over his monitor. When I confronted him about it, he reminded me that placing the monitor in his room had not been legal. Chagrined, I readily moved the camera out of his room. Sometimes, legality trumps convenience.

Fahy is handsome, no matter whether he's sporting a beard. He has blue eyes and fair hair, but he often dyes his hair dark red. He likes collecting clothes, owning a small shop's worth of clothes of various styles and colour. In putting them on, however, I have noticed he has a penchant for being a bit eclectic: although he has all kinds of socks, but he never wears two identical ones, lending him a peculiar appearance!

Fahy's background is no less colourful than his wardrobe. He was born in Ireland and has two sisters. As a youth, he lived in Holland for several years and, after he'd had enough of windmills and wooden shoes, immigrated to Canada at the age of nine – with his parents, I presume!

Oddly, he seldom cooks and showers in my home. I thank him for these actions (the hot water bill is no laughing matter in a city such as Toronto). *But does he eat, and if so, where?* I conclude that he must be eating well somewhere, as he proves to be full of strength when carrying several very heavy items in and out of his room. Clearly, he's been eating his spinach.

Today, Fahy's strength proves to be a Godsend, as he expertly carries Bo—complete with his carrier—to the vets for his annual injections. He even kisses Bo several times (only after I implore him to do so). Outer strength and inner compassion—with a friend such as Fahy, I was full of sorrow when he finally moved out after two years. The reason had been unsurprising: he had gotten a girlfriend. Diamonds in the rough may be hard to find, and can feel nothing but happiness for him and his new gal.

It's the Simple Things

Now it is autumn; the weather has turned cold. A late-October chill has descended on the city giving it a feeling that is not unlike winter, but, in fact, I still wear a dress—but with winter boots and a long jacket. I'm not daunted by the weather, and I happily take the TTC on a tour of Toronto. Today, I take the number 112 bus as evening gets underway. The driver has closed all the windows and blasted the heat, giving the bus a warm, cozy and quite comfortable feel. As cold and flu season approaches, it's reassuring not to hear a single cough from any of the passengers.

Who is our leader-behind-the-wheel on this fine crisp evening? Well, he's about five-ten, of average build, and possibly of Irish or Scottish stock. I like him already—and not just because I happen to be partial to blue eyes and fair hair! He gives the impression of genuinely caring about the passengers. Some drivers open several windows now and refuse to turn on the heat, creating the illusion that passengers are not on bus, but rather riding in a sleigh through the Rocky Mountains in the dead of winter. When I get on their buses I feel a constant chill. This driver, though, isn't shy about even *cranking* the heat up. It's so warm, in fact, that I cannot even put my leg on the heat any longer time, because, if I do, I'll feel a burning sensation. Nevertheless, in general, I appreciate the heat.

On this evening, it lulls me into a comfort zone which results in my staying on the bus for over four hours. But eventually, nature calls, and I have to visit the little girls' room. At the next stop, I get off the bus, but also notices that the driver does the same, standing in front of the bus, apparently on break. I notice that we're in a residential neighbourhood devoid of any public washrooms. Embarrassed, I return to my seat. *I cannot directly tell him I need to pee!* But, in motion again, another chance soon turns up as the bus pulls into Eglinton West Station. The driver scoots inside, but, not finding a public washroom in the building, I end up peeing directly on the pavement—you go girl! Feeling satisfied (if not a bit sheepish) I get back on the bus. Before long, the driver returns and—judging by the look of shock and bemusement plastered all over his face—notices what I have done. Mercifully, he seems to have understood that I hadn't a choice.

Continuing our merry way, I thoroughly enjoy this simple bus ride. The reassuring whir of the diesel engine as it accelerates after "rescuing" another waiting passenger from the cold and then settles into steady gear somehow allows me to calmly reflect on my blessings. Feeling grateful, after a rather lengthy sojourn we pull back into Eglinton West Station; the driver tells me he has finished driving the 112 for the day. It is no longer in service, meaning I could take the 32-bus home. So now, I soon get off the bus and notice that I must pee again. Why not go "aux naturel" once again? Finding a relatively quiet corner, I let her rip on the pavement (careful not to take care of business in the same place as before). *Ah, what a relief!* The 32 bus comes and on we go towards the subway station. I wait outside for the 63 for over half an hour, yet this (new) driver seems to be only sleeping! No longer able to stand the chilly weather, I take the subway home. Some people swear and walked away frustrated. But not me—I feel that today I was, in fact, fortunate to have taken 112 buses with that benign and kindly driver, showing people in his own quiet way that our community role models don't always have to be famous athletes or politicians.

The Next Generation

Today, I attended a Tibetan festival in the west end of the city. This was the first time, in fact, I had seen so many Tibetan monks and Tibetan people. With their toffee skin, sinewy yet solid physiques, and rich, dark hair they are easy to spot. I have come to greatly admire them. At the festival, I have the opportunity to see many Tibetan children's books, which I love very much. Yet, I do not understand the Tibetan language so I cannot gain much from buying them. What a pity. One black cat cartoon book looks inviting. *Will they ever create an English version?*

At this event, it's noon and we are treated to a free lunch. I notice that the monks all eat very quickly. I had bought two pork hoofs earlier and now I eat one of them and give the other to our temple's monk. But he declines, and some other monks dive in. They thank me profusely, claiming that the meat had been delicious. This makes me happy.

In the afternoon, some lovely Tibetan children put on a performance. Seeing them on stage eloquently singing and playing instruments, it's easy to admire them. One thing impresses me, in particular. Although Tibetan adults have unique features, as children—to me at least—they appear simply to be Asian children. The first song in their performance is 'Oh Canada'. The kids sing in English perfectly, but they also sing some songs in Tibetan. I see that their parents are proudly watching them, which makes me feel that the kids are incredibly lucky, happy, and secure. Although I have no children, the beauty and warmth of family is not lost on me, and for that, I feel blessed.

The Good TTC Driver

Tonight, I find myself wide awake once again. So, I go outside and hop on the TTC. I take the streetcar 506 from Dundas West, heading east. The driver, once again, is a good one, and kind, as well. He looks to be good-humoured and sincere. I like him already. Outside, the rain falls incessantly, its icy rivulets running across my window. The driver never chases anyone off the streetcar—something that you occasionally see in Toronto. Because he keeps the warm air flowing, I feel relaxed enough to be lulled into slumber. But I don't want to sleep. I want to take in the lively social interplay amongst the other riders, observe the driver's easy ability to field passengers' questions patiently and helps them get to their destinations. Somehow, these pleasant interactions make me believe that maybe, just maybe, all is right with the world—at least for now. When he arrives at Main Street Subway Station, he ducks into Tim Hortons for sustenance. Once again, nature calls, and this time I can't hold it. I feel embarrassed. The driver returns, but he doesn't get at all angry, for which I am eternally grateful. When he finishes his shift, I notice that he goes to McDonald's and buys a burger for one woman who, apparently, rides the streetcar day and night. She thanks him. He does not buy anything for himself. I hope that the TTC head office can give him an award for his kind service to all of us. His actions make me feel as if the TTC is, in a sense, my second home. As I depart the streetcar, feeling more at ease than I had when I jumped on it, I realize that I love Toronto—and the TTC. I'm not sure that I could live anywhere else.

Mervyn Johnston and I

Mervyn was my mentor. Before passing, he taught me how to invest in stocks, dealing with my stocks and seldom causing me to lose any money. This, in fact, has helped me live without financial difficulty. For this, I not only admire him, but I am also humbled by the kindness he showed me. Mervyn helped me revise my essays, allowing me to publish three books. I feel fortunate to have had him in my life.

It began innocuously enough. At the end of March, in 2024, Mervyn felt an ache in his belly and was suffering from a little constipation. With his niece accompanying him, he visited the hospital for testing, and was, before long, staring down a diagnosis of stomach cancer. Unbelievably, this ever-strong man immediately began to deteriorate. He refused to take fluids and couldn't stomach even soft food. He relied only on infusions to survive. In just half a month, he had lost 15 pounds. Three weeks after entering hospital, he found himself in palliative care.

During these three weeks, I went to the hospital many times. I brought him food, hoping to help lift his spirits. In the beginning, he was able to eat a little bit. But before long, he only wanted coffee and water. I also bring some gifts for his doctor. I even brought him a TTC pass to him in case he wanted to go home on his own. I had hoped that he could, before long, return home, even though, in my heart I knew that this wouldn't be happening. Unfortunately, his brother and family members weren't the kindest to me. They seemed to be overly protective. They told the hospital staff that, other than his family members, nobody should be allowed to visit him or to call him. As a result, everyone else—including me—lost contact with Mervyn. No doubt, his condition continued to deteriorate, I thought, and I felt helpless to do anything about it.

In my mind, Mervyn was an intelligent and strong role model. I could always rely on him, and he never let me down. He is so intelligent that he could kill it on weekly Jeopardy-themed matches at the university. I will, in my heart, love him and respect him always.

In his final days on this planet, I thought of him in his weakened state, unable perhaps to make clear decisions. All of his friends wanted him to recover. His family maintained that he would be best cared for in a nursing home or in the hospital, and Mervyn didn't disagree with them. *Holy Crap*, I thought, *He's really not going to recover!* Reality was setting in, as eventually, he couldn't get out of bed and was repeating the same sentences. I felt that he had already given up on the possibility of getting better, which, I felt, was a pity. Despondent, I swore I would never let this happen to me. My oh my, how time flies. He was a hero in my mind. I do not know why he collapsed so fast.

Mervyn taught me everything: how to study, how to write, even how to relax. He helped me in the garden. He reminded me when it was recycling day. He even helped me clean my yard and trimmed my rose bushes. He was my disciplinary.

Every Tuesday, it was our business lunch, usually dining at one of Mervyn's favourite places, KFC. I paid because Mervyn never charged me money for all the financial advice he gave me. Every week, I cooked or bought some delicious food and I let him come into my home to enjoy a dinner, which, I really believe, contributed to his happiness. I loved him just as I would a father.

Housing and Construction

The Toronto mayor wants to build more affordable housing in Toronto. I am doubtful it will really happen. Riding the TTC across the city, it's easy to observe there are many skyscrapers in Toronto, many of them with much unoccupied space. Venturing out in the evening, one can see many big buildings with only a few lights on. Even worse, other buildings, under construction, remain unfinished after five years.

If you take the 504 to the Distillery Loop, you will see there are nine tall condominium buildings. Yet, every time the streetcar stops there, only two or three people disembark. *Where are all the tenants?* The buildings have been standing for over ten years, but the place has the air of a ghost town. Travelling to the west end of the city, near Kipling Subway Station, one can see over twenty buildings, but you can count on your fingers on lights that are on at any given moment.

Consider, for a moment, my own sleepy little neighbourhood. One condominium has been built during the last three years. Nevertheless, for the most part, it is still empty, which makes me wonder, *is this a problem with the government's commitment to following through on their pledge to build more housing?* Privately, I implore the mayor and her council to find some way to solve this housing crisis. It's not rocket science, after all, is it?! With the plethora of recent constructions, it appears there is, now, enough living space for all of Toronto residents. Clearly, it must be mostly a matter of better distributing this living space so that all can have what is really a basic human right: having a roof over one's head.

For instance, if one walks around the city, it soon becomes apparent that, virtually everywhere, there is a construction site. But is this a wise solution for all of our urban space? The Eglinton and Yonge intersection has innumerable existing buildings, as well as construction sites, but it's taking forever to complete all of the infrastructure projects in the area, including the new subway line being built. One wonders, *is it all necessary? Does Toronto really want to be another New York City?* Who is going to pay for all this prestige and glory, in the end?

The Black Girl

Today, a young black girl saved my life. Attempting to get on the streetcar with my hands full, I lost my balance and almost fell. Suddenly though, I felt a strong hand on my back, supporting me from behind as I teetered toward the pavement. This allowed me to safely land on the road. I looked up and saw a surprisingly gentle and sweet face smiling at me benevolently. To say I was appreciative of the young woman's help would be an understatement. To top it off, she treated the whole situation like it wasn't a big deal. This the first time that I was saved in such a way. It gave me hope—if our future is in the hands of such youngsters, we'll be okay. With one simple action, a member of this new generation displayed respect, selflessness, and modesty. *Thank you, kind young woman.*

Broadview Hotel

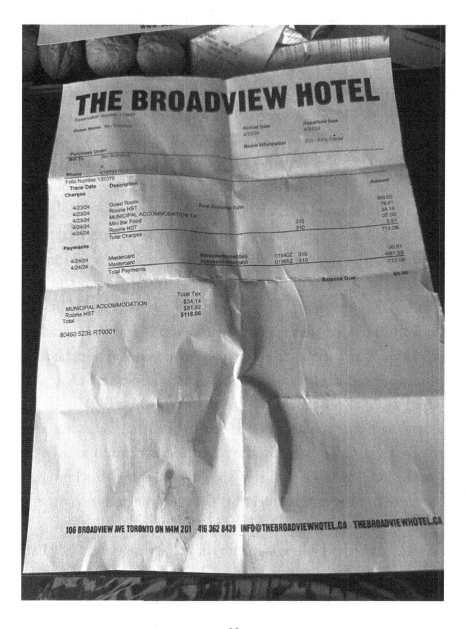

On April 23rd, 2024, I felt uncomfortable. I decided to find a hotel to live for one night. I checked online and found that near Yonge and Bloor, there were many good hotels where I could stay. However, one voice repeatedly told me that there would be no rooms left at this place. To make matters worse, I could not find any information on whether or not the other hotels had rooms. In the meantime, I did not want to live in a shabby room.

Finally, after some spirited searching, I found the Broadview Hotel in the city's somewhat rundown east end. I took the TTC to Broadview Subway Station. Then I called a taxi, which jettisoned me directly to the once grand old hotel. I entered the lobby and was astounded by how ridiculously small it looked from the inside. *Were people that much smaller 100 years ago than we are today?* One thing, though, was Okay with me: there was a bar behind the check-in room. "Good evening and welcome to the Broadview," croaked the reception desk clerk who, with his white whiskers and staid purple three-piece suit, looked old enough to be a permanent part of the hotel itself. I said that I wanted to reserve a second-floor, middle room. He informed me that only the third floor and fourth floor rooms were vacant. I chose the third floor (being a Chinese Canadian I avoid anything having to do with the number four), on which a suite was booked for me. The cost? A cool 682 dollars. My first reaction was to run. However, the old black-and-white clock on the wall indicated that it was already past 9 pm. I was ready to give up. It was so expensive that I thought I must have ordered a vice-presidential suite. I checked online and read the presidential suite cost a cool three thousand per night (meaning I had saved almost over two grand—oh joy, oh bliss!). After taking my key card, I ventured over to the elevator and found that I did not know how to use the card. To my disappointment, the receptionist refused to help me. But one thing was good—one man was also renting a room on the third floor and, thanks to his help, eventually I was able to get off the elevator and into my room.

On my floor, things seemed to be okay. Nevertheless, there was an eerie presence—as if a ghost had come into the room, which necessitated some action on my part. So, I began my inspection: there was a corridor leading into a bedroom. I went to the washroom first. It was good that the toilet was not dirty, at least. I was afraid to take a shower because I feared that the towel and nightgown would have sexually transmitted diseases. Although there was no water, I found that there were three bags of snacks, which I put in my bag. My room had three bearskins which, I could see, were made with real bear's fur. It was interesting—I love bears. But I did not want them to be killed, so I didn't take photos. I lay on a king size bed which was very soft. I turned on the TV, which showed only a hanging ghost picture. I changed the channels, but nothing happened. Tired, I shut it off and slept.

In the morning, I woke up with a start. At first, I could not walk—both of my legs could not stand straightly. I immediately checked out at the front desk, where I found that I could not get my deposit back. *Was I was being ripped off?* Forlornly, I made my way outside and noticed that the 501 streetcar had just pulled up to the stop not 20 metres from me. No time to get down about money. I jumped on it and went home, satisfied that, at the very least, I'd had a change of scenery.

Doctor Devanshu Desai

My psychiatrist Desai has seen me for over eight years. I like him, as he is very kind and compassionate. He has never lost his temper with me. Every time he sees me, he uses a soft voice, speaking to me with gentleness and genuine concern. He asks me about my daily life and helps me to solve problems—both mentally and physically. Once, when I went to the TDSB to study, he arranged free house cleaners for me. They came for over three months. This small—but very timely—act of kindness did not go unappreciated by this writer.

Doctor Desai is Indian. I wonder if his background speaks to his formality. He sometimes uses *extremely* professional language *(read: what are you saying, exactly, Doctor!?)* when speaking with me, but I'm not deterred. I know he's good. He takes care in writing prescriptions for me, reminding me never to exceed the recommended dosage and explaining to me, in detail, if necessary, of all the potential side effects. I like this.

Every year, Doctor Desai returns to India to visit his older brother. He has two children: a boy and a girl. He speaks English very well, and is a very busy man, since he oversees the whole clinic. He also treats his staff well. Most of them like him. He goes by the nickname, 'Doctor D'.

Once, I read a book about Doctor Freud, which claimed that he had whipped his cleverest patient, a Russian girl. They both felt pure, joy, and love, according to the book. This intrigued me, and I suddenly had an idea. I asked Doctor D if he could whip or spank me—I did not want to rely on the medications for my treatment because I feared they had too many side effects—and I wanted, in fact, to *cure* my mental illness. I wanted the good doctor to beat me instead of writing prescriptions for. Shocked by my admission, he refused to do so.

Consequently, I didn't go to the psychiatric hospital for over six years. Instead, I felt that I was simply lucky to be Doctor D's patient. I loved his care and counselling. He was one of my best psychiatrists and had a lot of patients. The fact that he was always quite busy didn't dissuade me from continuing to be his patient.

Doctor Desai teaches me how to deal with stress and anxiety. He encourages me to study and to be a useful person to others. What's more, I have learned how to behave myself around him. He has an Indian incense fragrance, containing a very pleasant smell which I like. He never wears overly luxurious clothes, which might intimidate his patients. Instead, being modest, he wears simple clothes and a pair of good shoes. He does not drive. He takes the TTC to his office. He does not look down upon us, instead treating us friendly, respectfully and equally. I have never met another psychiatrist like him.

On the other hand, to my view, Doctor Desai prescribes medications which are not very good. He too frequently uses very old medicines. He believes that new medications may have worse side effects.

I am Daddy's Little Doggy

I love my father. He is the number one dad in the world. Although not exactly blonde, he is white. I am his only son. He stands about five feet, nine inches tall, and I come only to his waist. My mom is a black woman from Africa. She has dark coloured skin and eyes. To be honest, I do not like her so much.

My dad likes to kiss me. He kisses my head, my face, and lips. Of course I love to kiss him too. He pampers me all the time. He often buys candies for me, although he is not rich.

We take the TTC all the time to go to school. He often brings me on a detour which allows me to enjoy more scenery. I love it very much.

I am a young boy, but Daddy is a big man. He talks to me all the time and gives me endless love. My mother did not marry my father. In fact, both do not wear wedding rings on their fingers. My mom does the housework. She always watches us, but seldom talk talks to my dad. She is full of deep self-pity. She thinks of her dark skin colour and the face that I look like her—not like my dad. My dad never beats me. He likes to tease me and encourages me to study.

He kisses me just like he was kissing a little doggy. I like it. That is why I say that I am Daddy's little doggy.

Mervyn Johnston

MERVYN EDWARD JOHNSTON

In loving memory of Mervyn Edward Johnston, born on April 9, 1949, and departed from this world on April 18, 2024. Mervyn's life was a testament to kindness and selflessness, as he dedicated himself to helping others and finding joy in everyday moments. He was preceded in death by his father, Harold; mother, Phyllis; and sister, Brenda; but leaves behind a legacy of compassion and wisdom that will be cherished by his brother, Rick, sister-in-law, Frances, and nieces, Amanda, Kasia, and Melanie. A private family celebration of Mervyn's life will take place in the summer of 2024, honoring his belief that "Life's purpose is to enjoy each day in some way," and his guiding principle that "Decisions are important - others should benefit from them, it shouldn't be just about yourself." May Mervyn rest in peace, knowing that his legacy of kindness and generosity will continue to inspire those he touched throughout his life. Online condolences may be made through: www.turnerporter.ca

Turner & Porter

Mervyn Johnston was born on April 9th, 1949, and passed away on April 18th, 2024. He was a brilliant stockbroker and a multimillionaire. He was also my mentor during the time that he corrected my essays. He had faith in my writing, telling me to aim high: focus on winning an Oscar and the Nobel Prize. I was delighted when my debut book was published. Yet, I did not win any awards. I am a Canadian writer who competes with US writers, which makes writing a commercially successful book very challenging.

Mervyn's house was akin to storage room—it had all kinds of books, DVDs and blue rays. He shopped for these things twice every week. Some books and DVDs were very rare and expensive. Every Christmas and on my birthday, he gave me some blue rays, which I still love today. I thanked him every single time I saw him.

Mervyn was a saver. Every time he went to Walmart, he bought barbequed chicken for half price. He bought copies of the same sweater when they had a big discount. He even bought the same pair of shoes four times. When one shoe was broken, he simply replaced that one. I felt that he was too cheap. Mervyn always rode a bicycle—even in winter. If there was no rain or snow, he rode his bike faithfully.

Mervyn listened to the stock reports every day. He also subscribed to Stock Money Magazine for decades. When it came to finance, he knew what was doing.

Mervyn had no children, but he gave me a father's love. He cared about me all the time. We often accompanied each other on outings. We got our COVID 19 vaccinations together, with him being considerate enough to book the appointments for us both. He often helped me to buy milk, since Shoppers Drug Mart discounted it for seniors on Thursdays. I liked to drink milk, and he knew it.

Every time I went to his house, he served me coffee and hot chocolate. He always stood while making them, passing them to me gently, careful to make sure I didn't burn my hand on the hot mug. When I asked him to sit down, he said that if he sat down, he wouldn't be able to stand up again. *What a character!* Regardless, I liked to sit down for hours. Mervyn gave me a second childhood, and for that, I will love him forever.

In my mind, my natural father seldom took me places. I lacked parents' love. I think that was the main reason I loved Mervyn so much.

Mervyn was afraid of animals, especially dogs. It's funny because I love animals and, for years, had a giant dog, a King Sheppard. He never touched King.

Mervyn made salads every day. He liked to eat salads. Profusely. Carnivorous, I didn't like salads at all. I often joked with him about this contrast in our characters. I am higher than you in the food chain, I told him. He laughed at that.

Mervyn Johnston is forever my mentor, my father and my best friend. I love him forever.

Hot Apollo

I met Hot Apollo on the TTC bus. I had not heard of him before I saw him. He was super thin. I knew that he could strip dance because he had special lungs. I gave him five dollars for tips, but he refused to take anything. So, I gave him twenty dollars, and he accepted that. He stood beside me and asked me what I wanted to. When he invited me to listen to his concert, I told him that I did not like the concert, but I liked his dancing. He was silent and passed me his business card. I saw that it said, "Hot Apollo." I asked him if he could strip dance for me. He said that indeed he could. He had tattoos on his body and hands, and I touched them. Seemingly taken aback, he hid his hands. One of his friends, who wore a fox fluffy mask, was real joker. Hot Apollo invited me to the concert to which, apparently, all of his friends were going to, but I refused. On the bus later, we decided that he would go to my home to dance, then he got off the bus and went to his show that Saturday night.

I went home. The following Wednesday, I called him. However, he only sent texts to me, which made me believe he was only playing games with me. I was despondent that he had given me a bunch of baloney—he had not shown up as agreed upon. Angry, I told him that he was a liar and hung up the phone.

Out of curiosity, I searched for him online. He played rock music, but it wasn't my thing. He was actually good enough to go on the show 'Canada's Got Talent'. He sang his best song, yet all four referees failed him. Anyway, he had tried.

Hot Apollo might have had a drug addiction, since his body was practically a bag of bones. I knew how hard it was to lose weight. I listened to his songs online. I found that he always wore weird clothes, whether he was on the stage or not. He often bared his upper body and, on his bottom, he wore only short shorts. He was dancing and singing very strangely, and it was hard to understand what he was doing. Also, he had a funny voice. He really needs to retire, since he did not have enough of an audience and his commercial performance were too limited. Strangely, in spite of his miserable treatment of me, I empathized, as I knew that it was very hard to be a musician.

Today, I occasionally check on Hot Apollo. He is still singing, and recently, he had a brand new release. Good luck to him.

Buddy's Birthday

I gave Buddy away over three years ago, but I will never forget him. He is forever my kid. His birthday is coming, and I'll still prepare birthday gifts for him.

Buddy's new owner is a farmer and an animal lover too. I am pretty happy that he adopted my dog. Also, my neighbour knows him and often helps me deliver food and other things to Buddy. Today, I bought five big bags of dog food, two large bags of treats, and two big size bottle of dog mouth wash for his all the owner's dogs. He has four dogs in total. As a dog mom, I just hope that Buddy will have a great life and John, Buddy's new owner, loves Buddy even more than I do.

I haven't had Buddy's videos or photos for a long time. I messaged John many times but got no response. I knew that either one, he was busy or, two, he simply did not want me to contact him and Buddy anymore. Yet a mother's love cannot stop me from doing so. He is forever mine. I cannot forget him, so much so that today, I am trying to find a boyfriend who can drive me to visit Buddy. I expect experience this angst for years. When Buddy left me, I adopted three cats to compensate for not having Buddy in my life. Now, though, I feel my money is a little bit tight. I have to go to the food bank for help. Yet, I make sure that my cats still eat the best cat food ('Blue Buffalo Wild') out there. Buddy's dog food was 'Purina One', which was also a famous brand. But not cheap. All of these thoughts of my pets made me reflect on how I had lost Buddy. The clincher, really, had been when my dad informed me that he would not be sending me money any longer. Nevertheless, I do not regret either adopting these pets or spending half of my income on them, as I love animals. I even feed the raccoons near my house. I feel that I am a mom to all of them.

I bought some decent clothes for John, and for his neighbour who helped with his care, as a show of thanks for caring for Buddy. I think they are happy about this. I am happy too—and I hope that Buddy still remembers me.

Dr. Wood's Retirement

Dr. Michael Wood retired on May 7th, 2024, just shy of his 80th birthday. Now, it feels like my heart is broken. He was my knee specialist. He cured my knee pain and gave me a father's love and for those things, I will not forget him.

He had been my doctor for three years and I grew to love him. He had blue eyes that were so beautiful, so pure. His eyes were like blue rays of sunshine that lit my heart and made humbled me. His voice was a kind of melody: powerful, yet unforgettable. His clothes were simple. He wore an operating uniform, a t-shirt and pants, always with running shoes. When I saw him, I felt that he touched my heart each time we met. Because he was a doctor and I was his patient, I realized that I should not have invaded his privacy in any way, so I simply kept quiet and left it for my imagination. I hid my love and my curiosity. I hated my parents; after all, they did not take care of me very well and consequently, I suffered. I have dreamt, in fact, that I am Dr. Wood's child and that I see him every day and live with him for good. Dr. Wood told me that he had two sons and no grandchildren. I imagine that they are still young, since Dr. Wood finished his doctorate degree and got his licence in 1979 and 1980.

I am the only person in my family who lives in Canada. All my relatives are in China. Every time I miss my father, I will tell myself that Doctor Wood is my daddy. In fact, in my mind, I sometimes say that several times and cry myself to sleep. *Who will help me in this new country? I do not know.* I just hope that Doctor Wood will read my books and remember me. Because I love him, that hope is enough.

Once, Doctor Wood said that he had wife. I have tried to forget him, but I cannot. Actually, I saw Doctor Wood over one hundred times, in total. Sometimes we just met for five or ten minutes. His professional skills moved me deeply. His good temper and gentle love made a deep impression on me. He had a dog, but he never showed me the photos. By way of contrast, I always showed pictures of my four cats to him, and it pleased me when he said that he liked them. Once Dr. Wood wore a Tommy Hilfiger sweater with a lot of dog fur on it, which made me laugh.

Wood was a slim man. He always told me that I should lose weight and walk more. But I am a little bit lazy. Dr. Wood is left-handed. He believed that being left-handed is a sign of intelligence, but I often said it was a sign of laziness!

When Dr. Wood told me that he would retire. I ask him, "After I publish my fourth book how I can give it to you?" He said simply, "Bring it to the office, I'll be waiting for it!" Every time I think that I could not see Dr. Wood anymore, it fills me with sadness. He was such a good doctor that he even remembered my phone number and my address. Yet, really, I barely knew him. I feel slighted.

In my heart, Doctor Wood is forever my father.

China Chin Hot Pot and BBQ Toronto

Today I felt hungry, so I found myself at the China Chin restaurant to eat at the buffet. I sat down and ordered a pot of mushroom soup. To my surprise, they gave me a spicy pot but when I put the food in it, I found that it was a pot that somebody had already ate from. I knew this because there was a lot of dirty soup, and it had not boiled for a long time. I ordered lamb, which they served me. I put the lamb in the pot and tasted it. I was shocked. It was not lamb at all. I knew this because, as a meat lover, I have eaten all kinds of meats, including pork, chicken, rabbit, lamb, beef, dog, donkey, horse, and deer. I had never eaten this meat. The taste was strange to me, and it had a little bit of a mutton smell but not at all a lamb one. As I looked at it, I saw dark red meat, with a white circle around the outside. I had never seen that kind of lamb at all, and it was the first time I tasted it. A horrific image flashed through my mind as I considered, *could it be human meat?* I immediately became frightened and asked the waiter to change the meat, but she refused. Shocked, I did not eat and simply paid the bill and left. Now, I fear this Chinatown restaurant. I'm convinced that they sell human meat. Suffice to say, I will not go to this restaurant anymore.

Halloween Cats 11

This year it is the first year that my four cats got together on Halloween. Their names are Prince, Bo, Kinder and Milo, and they're my kids. Bo always bullies Prince, so Prince just stays in my room. I adopted Prince almost twelve years ago. Bo, who is five, originally was my tenant's cat. I bought Kinder and Milo from the same breeder. Kinder, the only female, is three years old, and Milo is almost two years old. They are Siamese. I love all of them, Prince is my favourite.

Prince likes to play with cat toys on my bed. Today, I bought a big black rat toy for him. He works hard, playing with it. The other cats spend a lot of time in the living room, chasing each other and making love together. Bo savagely bites Kinder's neck and makes love to her—doggie style! Kinder sometimes cooperates with Bo; but sometimes she appears to be angry and turns on him. Milo knows that he is the lowest cat on the totem pole. He is permitted to only *occasionally* mate with Kinder.

But getting back to Halloween: First things first, I gave out candy to the kids, then I was simply at home watching my cats. Bo was extremely excited. He jumped on window ledge and fought with Jonny, the neighbour's cat, behind the glass window. Bo, really, is like a 'cat terrorist' in my house. Since he has long, shiny, black fur, on this special day I treated him very nicely. I gave him many cat treats to make up his trick or treats. Prince, who has short, black fur, likes to rest in my bedroom. This Halloween, I woke him up and played with him. Since he liked to sit on top of me, I knew I was satisfying him. I asked him what he wanted. He purred and he actually said *Ma*. This told me that he really missed me, and that he was an obedient cat. In fact, he is my favourite cat—I think of him like I would, I imagine, a first-born son.

I like Siamese cats. Kinder, though, is a character. When she first came to my home, she refused to eat. This went on for six months! She would look at the cat food and run, which puzzled me. Now, knowing that she is the only female cat in my home, she has, little by little, developed priorities: She eats first, mates with the tomcat of her choice and sometimes fights with all of them. Today, she is dynamic. Her beautiful blue eyes and black face make her charming and fashionable. Milo is just over a year old. He is a naughty boy and is my most affectionate cat. In fact, he loves everybody and greets everyone who he meets—and everybody loves him in return. Today, he is very lively and full of energy. He chases Bo and mates with Kinder. He runs quickly all over the house. He likes to have his photo taken, and so I take several pictures of him. These create some of the best memories I can imagine for both of us.

I do not let any of my cats go out of my house, since I fear I'll lose them. And the fact that it was Halloween reminded me that there are still some people who do not like black cats and will try to kill them. Home is, for me and my cats, truly a *sweet* home. My cats all understand this and play together for fun.

On Halloween, Bo wielded his paws to scare Prince and Milo, indicating that he wanted to be a centre of the special day. Prince jumped onto my dressing table and opened his mouth, raising his backbone as a scare tactic. "Come on, I realize that today is Halloween, but guys, please keep the peace," I said to them. Bo also jumped on my bed and Milo immediately went on the attack. In Milo's mind, Bo is vicious and unpredictable. "Bo, I love you." I said to Bo. He walked to eat his food. He had scratched his last owner's eyes, even blinding him temporarily. Hence, I did (and do) not like Bo on my bed. The consequence of this was that I bought a big cat mattress for him, which cost me 80 dollars. Kinder kissed Prince again. Prince licked her fur, hoping for a reward. They seldom make love—it is just like a father and daughter's relationship.

I love black cats, whether it's Halloween or not. I believe that people with cats have more longevity than non-cat owners, because we all have nine lives. 'Love me, love my cats'—that is my motto.

I made "Rose" and "Cat"

Pable Picasso

Pable Picasso was Spanish artist. He was famous all over the world. Yet I, for one, don't revere him.

He was a genius but also, he was, allegedly, a criminal. In some circles, he is thought to have killed many innocent women and students. And let's consider his sculpture. No one would forget his acrobatic female sculptures. They were in very different poses, yet they all had a very big, hooked nose which I never saw with other artists. Once, I saw a young man who had such a big nose. I asked him if he knew Picasso. He said that yes and claimed that the artist had destroyed all of his ancestors and tortured them to death, that he had even used their bodies to mold his sculptures. *Beyond horrible*, I thought.

Let's consider his other sculptures. One sculpture simply had two iron sticks protruding from his mistresses' breasts. He said that her breasts were the only part that he liked. This same sculpture had just two legs. Additionally, Picasso painted "an idiot". A lot of people think that he had good observational skills. But I believe he beat the head of a good man's skull, which led to many scattered broken bones. That the man had internal bleeding and injuries which made him feel just like a pot was sitting on top of his head, and that he was forever disabled. Then, Picasso drew a painting to show the vanquished state of his victim.

Picasso married a Spanish princess, but he still felt that she was not perfect enough for him and divorced her. Picasso claimed that his works could take up the whole gallery, but which other well-known artists couldn't say this? During the same era, another brilliant artist was Georges Braque, the French artist, who liked his students and had a gentle, kindly demeanor. His works also occupied a whole gallery.

Stephen Goodwin's Biography

Stephen Goodwin was my English teacher. I admired him for a long time, and one semester, in fact, I chose his class. In the first class, he introduced himself. Turned out that had not attended university since he had been 35. He was born in Sault Ste. Marie, Ontario, Canada, on August 29th, 1965. After graduating from high school, he had become a singer and composer. When he was 21 years old, he went to Toronto, Ontario, but his career was not that successful. He was not that popular, although he often had some commercial musical performances. His original songs were seldom known by people. Attending York University, he earned a bachelor's degree and eventually got his master's from Queen's University. After that, he went back to college to obtain teaching certificate. Today, he has three sisters and two brothers and is a middle child. Stephen is very kind, his youngest sister being one of his biggest admirers. He's single and has no children. His eldest sister has three children. They are all well-educated.

He is slim, so he wears a size "M". He has said that his body's metabolism has some problems and that's why he's thin. His nose is exactly like his sisters', big and beautiful. He likes his name, Goodwin, which, he says, always inspires him to be good and to be a positive influence on others. He is very funny. He told me that he has many friends and that he had worked in the entertainment field for over 16 years; I imagine that his good looks must have attracted a lot of young women. Stephen was a good high school student, yet once he was very worried about his mathematics' score, so he went to see his mathematics' teacher to ask for his mark. The teacher said, "I can let you pass, but you must promise me one thing: you cannot choose math anymore." He agreed. So, the teacher gave him a 50 percent score for his math. This was, in fact, his last time studying math. Since he is not good at math, today he needs a family accountant to help him with the books. Every time his accountant wants to talk to him, he says to the accountant, "Please talk to me just like you would talk to a four-year-old."

Stephen likes electronic war games. He keeps on playing, until finally he becomes champion and the screen displays, "Welcome to the Army!" He enjoys this feeling. Stephen is against racism and race-based discrimination. He often reminds me *Bin; you should not think like a white supremacist.* If you want to be a popular writer, you should believe that everybody is equal. Stephen said that his handwriting is beautiful, but I joked with him, *in your dreams!* I like his handwriting because it's readable, elegant even.

On this day, at school, I want to go home soon. I rush to go, and he says, "Bin do you want to go home now? If so, you need to sign out first. That is the school's rule." So, I say to him, "I make my own rules." He blames me and says, "Do you want to go to jail?" *Is he joking?* He must be, yet I am still upset. So, I sign out and leave. Now, while in the class, I always watch Stephen. I wish that he could slap me on the spot. He said, "Do not use your eyeballs so strongly—they are burning my hands!" Once, I asked Stephen how many languages he could speak. He said two: English and body language.

The TTC Night Bus

The TTC night bus drivers are more often women than men. However, my thoughts are that, because nighttime is more dangerous than daytime, there actually should be more male drivers.

I like taking night buses. In general, I find that lady drivers are more efficient than their male counterparts, as they are more tolerant, and they can smooth out a bad situation. Also, they are more careful than male drivers. They know that this job opportunity is precious, and, hence, they cherish it a lot. I like their attitude and I hope that they can work in their jobs for a long time. And if I ever buy a second-hand bus, I'll make sure that it is a *lady-driven* one.

Police 12 Division Community Activity

Today is June 9th, 2024. I went to a Police 12 Division Community activity, which was open to public invitation.

I went there and thought that it was nothing special, but I do like free hamburgers and water, so I was able to, at least, take advantage of that. Then, I found some free water tanks and helped myself. Just one game, among all the games I played, offered a prize. I won a five-dollar gift card for the grocery store FreshCo, which I was over-the-moon to receive (near my home, is one of their outlets, where I often go for shopping). The whole east section of the police division consisted of children's games, and all this activity made me realize that I was very hungry. So, I went back to ask for a second hamburger, but the officers were eating and refused to give me seconds. I was furious and went to another booth. Suddenly, one police officer, who was wearing a turban, and one civilian, rushed me. They pushed and pulled my arms, twisting them grotesquely. They forced me to leave the station, holding my two arms in a V-shape. The civilian even twisted my wrist very painfully. When he grabbed my left breast, I yelled a warning at him, but it was no use. They pushed me all the way to the bus stop and swore at me, imploring me to leave. Thinking of the possibility of resulting injuries, I took their photos.

That was the police party I attended on that day.

Wok & Roast Chinese BBQ Restaurant

In East Toronto's Chinatown, Wok & Roast Chinese BBQ Restaurant is my favourite restaurant. Not only is the food very delicious, but also the boss is very nice.

The restaurant is open from 9 am to 9:30 pm, from Monday to Sunday. The most famous dish, BBQ pork, is out of this world, very delicious, and unforgettable.

I often go there to buy their BBQ pork. The tastiest part is the pig's feet. It is just $1.50 for one. Their BBQ Pipa duck also very delicious. They have so many dishes which are famous. The fried shrimps are very fresh and taste sweet. And I'm enamoured with the Bean Cure. If you eat it even once, you'll order it again.

The boss is kind and skillful. He buys coffee for his employees every morning. He buys XL sized coffee for his employees and small size coffee for himself. He always chops BBQ pork for his customers, cuts the bad pork off, and sells the good parts to customers. I remember that when I had bought a big chunk of BBQ pork in *another* restaurant, and they had given me all the bones.

Last year, at our church Christmas party, I ordered the whole BBQ pork from Wok & Roast Chinese BBQ Restaurant and the whole thing was eaten up in no time.

I like the fried lobsters. I remembered that, when I had been married to my late husband, we had ordered four big lobsters, and the boss had cooked them very cleanly—they were quite tasty. He had even given us five lobsters, instead of the four that I had ordered, to please us. My wedding banquet had been very successful. Even today, I still cannot forget it. *Thank you!* What's more, I liked the BBQ chicken legs and braised chicken legs. Even my dog often stole them.

The boss is very clean. He uses a special machine to clean his wood chopping board and wipes the kitchen counters all the time. He often washes his hands too.

The food is delicious, the prices are inexpensive, and these are the main reasons the restaurant is popular. Plus, the boss never cheats the customers and always thinks about us. I love this restaurant, and I will support it forever.

My English Teacher Michael

I found an English teacher whose name is Michael. He is great. I like him very much. He is intelligent and hardworking. He works at a business magazine and part time as an English teacher. His grammatical proficiency is brilliant. My broken English essays, under his correction, are much improved. I believe that for such great favour we should not simply say thanks. So, I bought some Chinese food as a show of gratitude. I think about giving him tips; however, I am not rich enough—and he'd likely refuse to take them anyway. He charges me very reasonable rates, which, I feel, is super-fair. He has both ability and integrity, which are rare to have in our modern society. His computer skills are also impressive. He corrected my essays very quickly and handily.

Michael is blonde and has blue eyes, which I find kind of attractive. I told him: "I love you." He has fair features and I imagine, in the strong Toronto summer sun, he can turn into a tomato quickly. I feel that he is a lucky gentleman and deserves a good wife to be with him for good. I feel that I cannot match him.

He is funny and often rides a bicycle to my home. My home is near his home—just 15 minutes by bike, in fact. His home is very clean and well-organized. My home, on the other hand, is not so clean all the time, but Michael doesn't mind at all.

He likes my cats and can even remember their names. There are four of them: two that are purely black and two, pure Siamese. Sometimes, even I am unable to tell them apart.

Strangely, Michael doesn't like his head exposed under a blowing fan. I guess that he must have overused his brain! I prefer male instructors. He is one of my favourite teachers. I love him.

This reminds me that I will never forget my mentor Mervyn Johnston, who taught me to focus on achieving the highest writing standards possible. I believe that, with Michael's assistance, I can reach these goals.

Today it is Father's Day. I invited—with sincerity in my heart—Michael to Chinatown to eat out, but he refused to go, as he's married. I was hurt. He texted me: "Good night, Bin."

My Beloved Husband

My late husband was a good joke teller. He often said some jokes to the people around him. Once he told me two fries and the shit' joke, I laughed a lot. He also told me something is funny, for example: in his factory, there was an engineer whose name was Danny. His skills were not too great. My husband once sang to him, "oh, Danny boy the pipes pipes are calling …". The engineer was very angry.

Since he liked to tell jokes to people, they also liked to fool him. Once he went to hospital for his back pain, the doctor saw his name and asked him what kind of job he did. He said security. The doctor said that: "Hi you are really Dennis Miners." Our surname is pronounced "sub junk" we all told people our name pronounced "subject". We did not like people calling us "sub junk" either.

Dennis had a good friend who taught him how to do leather work. In our home, we have a lot leather tools and all kinds of stamps. Some are very rare. His father even made some unique tools for him to make leather work. Unfortunately, his friend passed away. He had not done leather work for years.

My late husband was very kind. One of his neighbours often borrowed money from Dennis. He did not like it, yet he lent it to him. This neighbour call Dennis "an angel" sometimes, he never returned the money. Dennis lent 5000 dollars to his factory's woman worker in 1990s. She did not return even a cent.

Dennis could dance Ukrainian traditional folk dance well. When he was young, his parents sent him to Ukrainian dancing school to study. He sometimes danced for me. I love it so much.

Dennis loved cats. He did not like dogs. He went to the humane society to adopted Harry a male tabby cat. Harry was just tried to be put down, because he was very aggressive and attacked humans. Dennis could not see a cat being killed.

He immediately adopted Harry and brought him to the vet Saini. Vet Saini did the examination of Harry. He was in good shape. He neutered Harry. Dennis brought Harry home and was very happy. Harry clawed Dennis's legs causing bleeding. Everybody saw Dennis's legs. They all wanted him to give up Harry. He refused to do so. He loves Harry just like his elder son. After half a year, Harry did not claw Dennis too much anymore. Harry died when he was 19 years old.

Dennis liked music. As a reward, I often played Chinses classic songs to him. He did not understand Chinese, yet he liked the tunes. I was very glad to provide Chinese culture to him.

My late husband was very kind to me and others. Before I married with my late husband, my nose was bleeding when I ate food. After we were married, we ate in the restaurants, and I cooked delicious food. My nose never bled anymore. When I am eating, just a little bit snot discharges. I appreciate him forever. He saved my life. I love him forever.

The Underworld Fight with the Police

Toronto Police 12 Division had a community party on June 9th, 2024. Unexpectedly, in this dream, it became the underworld fight with the police.

Even though I had been expelled from the police station, there were still many civilians and police, from other police stations, inside. Many police cars drove here and there, and soon the atmosphere was chaotic. The police officers suddenly rushed into the station's women's washroom. Mafias were occupying the men's washroom. The police, of course, were armed with guns and other fatal weapons, but the gang leaders were lacking them. Consequently, the police found that they might not be able to handle the gangsters; they opened the women's door and fired into the men's washroom. They swore at their counterparts: "Come out or die!" Their opponents had one heavy weapon. Gradually, they opened the men's washroom door and, as soon as it was open, immediately fired into it. From the lady's washroom could be heard people's blood-curdling screams. Of course, some police died in this gunfight. No wonder they had fired their guns first.

Toronto Police 12 Division was a small police division and thus, they did not have their own weapons storage room. So, they called 11 Division and told them what happened, pleading for help. The 11 Division Superintendent, whose name was Andrew, could tell that this was serious and called some elite members who were heading there. However, he decided to drive the police car, 11S1, to 12 Division. To his dismay, he found that a Cougar (car) had stopped outside of 11 Division. Sitting in the car was the mafia leader. The superintendent knew that it was very dangerous situation, hence he changed his mind and called the patrol police at 12 Division to help, and he contacted Headquarters.

Coincidentally, Inspector Joyce's third husband was on duty. Even he did not believe what Andrew had said, but, without hesitating, called 12 Division. They confirmed that they needed help. In turn, Joyce's husband called 14 Division to help, who greed to be of immediate assistance. According to police, the Mafioso in the building were all now under control and would be killed because they had slaughtered police officers. Outside the building, the other gangsters and families were all under pressure. The wife of the mafia leader of the local neighbourhood was worried about her husband, who was in the station. She promised that the police, who she in fact controlled, could release the hostages, but only as part of an exchange. The police accepted, but they said that they needed a go-between. She recommended herself. Before she had gone, one of the leader's concubines wanted to replace her, since it was too risky. The police, however, never followed their promise in their fight with the gangsters. She refused to allow the concubine to go in, and instead, ran into the station herself.

All areas of the building, other than the washrooms, in fact, had warning alarms. She hesitated at first but went into the ladies' washroom. The outside door had already been half destroyed. She just wanted to talk; one door opened, and a police officer poked her with handgun. She did not carry weapons because she was afraid of causing a misunderstanding. In response to her actions, one police officer pressed a knife against her throat and threatened her, imploring that her husband must give up. Suddenly, she knew that she had been taken in. The police told her husband that if he did not follow their orders, she would be killed immediately. The black hands also thought that if he was arrested, his associates would kill the police who were under their control and fight to rescue their leader—there would be so many losses. But he did not come out. The police ended up cutting his wife's throat, hand-cuffing her inside the closet. Blood spewed everywhere. The victim's husband had not ordered the killing of the police hostages. Instead, he wanted to talk about a peaceful settlement, yet the police refused. Fifteen minutes passed; blood flooding the floor, she died. It was pure murder.

However, this story had not finished. The gangsters fought with the police, which enabled the leader to escape, sprinting outside amidst a flurry of bullets. The police, seeing that he had left, agreed to release the gangsters, who let the police who had been captured return to safety. It seemed that, in a manner of speaking, everything had been solved. Yet the gang leader was in extreme pain. He swore that, in the future, he would kill the police who had murdered his wife.

Printed in the United States
by Baker & Taylor Publisher Services